Copyright

8-26-18

Thank you for selecting 'Lucky Seven'. A young minister goes to Viet Nam and receives the gift of healing, and then loses it. It is a story of redemption. A very powerful story.

Other Stories:

1. "Bodhi" a Sci-Fi series (8 books) deals with aliens from another dimension, Black hole, and what is on the other side of the veil (death).
2. "Rose" a series (16 books) the adventures of a twelve-year-old girl on the Mississippi River (1830) and the Indian plains.
3. "Ana" A very intense story of a young Jewish girl (14 years) surviving the Nazi prison camps, love, and war, written in narrative poetic style.
4. "Buffalo Boy" A young man of twelve is cast away from his village and forced to live with the buffalo.
5. "Detective Harriet Brown:" This a series of detective stories around a young lady in her early twenties.
6. "Jason" A young man possessed with a beast within learns to survive in Los Angeles after the great Earthquake, and the release of a deadly virus.

Lucky Seven

By Christopher Charles

Content:

Prolog

I was attending an Easter Sunrise service at the local college's football field. I sat in the bleachers facing a twenty-foot roped off aisle that ran all the way across the grass to the stage. People with blankets were either side sitting on chairs or on the grass listening to the choir. The sun had begun to peek through the clouds. We were all standing singing a song with the choir.

A man dressed as a street person was working his way towards the stage carrying a bouquet of lilies. He passed in front of us and started walking down the twenty-foot wide aisle towards the stage. Ushers were running after him. Two of them reached him and dragged him back towards the entrance.

Immediately I felt this surge of energy come over me as I fell back into my seat. I could not move for a moment. Finally, the major part of the energy released me allowing me to function, but a small amount remained until I had written this story. I still become very emotional when I read it.

1 South Vietnam

It was the year 1964 on an airbase pad in South Vietnam. Four helicopters were being loaded with US Army soldiers. Captain Bollinger, career soldier, medium built, on the ground watched from another pad of four helicopters that were also being loaded. When everyone was aboard, he raised his hand and whirled it. The four helicopters on the first pad lifted off.

Captain Bollinger walked to his helicopter. When he was aboard, the quad of helicopters lifted off and followed the other helicopters out over the jungle.

On a third pad was Lieutenant Jones, a short medium built man, leaned against a single helicopter with big number seven printed on its side smoking a cigarette. He watched the helicopters disappear over the horizon.

Christopher Charles

His co-pilot leaned out the open door and yelled, "Shouldn't we be getting along sir,"

"Yeah, right," He took one more strong puff of smoke into his lungs and then flipped the cigarette from his fingers. He turned and climbed into the helicopter. "I'm getting the hell out of this man's army tomorrow. I'm tired of these suicide missions."

"You're lucky, I've got another year," his copilot said as Jones took the helicopter into the air.

Lieutenant Smith, a big shoulder man, in the lead quad of helicopters looked out the windscreen at the jungle fifteen hundred feet below. He spoke through his helmet mike, "Field of lilies up ahead, sir, should be there in five."

Captain Bollinger spoke into his helmet mike, "The count was two hundred a mile south of it. The information's two hours old."

The jungle suddenly opened up revealing five acres filled with white lilies. It was the only clear area for the helicopters to land for twenty miles around.

Lucky Seven

Lieutenant Smith spoke through his helmet mike, "Yes sir, I see the clearing now."

"You're in first, Smith," Captain Bollinger said over the speaker, "We'll follow on the east side. Good luck! Let's get a good body count today."

The long stems of the white lilies moved back and forth in the wind. They were closed except for a few in full bloom. In the distance four helicopters approached and landed in the middle of the field. The men inside emerged quickly and took up positions around the helicopter away from the rotating blades.

From the jungle gunfire erupted. A missile streaked across the lily field and struck one of the helicopters attempting to take off. The helicopter exploded in place and falls to the ground.

Lieutenant Smith watched the last of his men jump off the helicopter and yelled into his helmet mike, "We've been set up! It's a trap! Jack took one. I'm getting the hell out of here."

Two bullets ripped through Smith's windscreen and buried themselves in the seat beside him. He pulled back on the stick taking the helicopter up. In the distance he saw a missile approaching fast. Calmly, he said, "Missile incoming, I'm taking one."

The helicopter exploded in the air as the other two helicopters lifted off and escaped out over the jungle.

Below, in the field, a strong black man, Sergeant Meade, stood and yelled at his men, "Move it, or die here! Your ride's gone!"

The soldiers followed Meade's charge across the clearing with their guns blazing. The return fire was intense. Several men were hit and dropped to the ground. The remaining men along with Meade found cover at the edge of the clearing, and tucked in.

Sergeant Meade turned to see the wounded men trying to crawl up behind him and yelled "Stay where you are!" He pulled out the mike from his radio pack and spoke into it, "We got wounded. The clearing's secured."

Lieutenant Jones picked up the radio transmission, and said, "It's our turn to pick up the pieces." He dropped his helicopter lower and moved across the jungle fifty feet below him. He saw the burning helicopters on the ground, and

Lucky Seven

Sergeant Meade waving at him to land between them and the edge of the clearing.

He swung his helicopter around and banked it over the spot. When he was twenty foot off the ground, two slugs pierce the windshield striking his co-pilot in the chest and the other one embedded itself in the seat beside his head. He yelled into the mike, "You call this secure!"

He pulled back on the stick and pushed the throttle hard. The helicopter banked to the left exposing its engine. He managed to gain two hundred feet when five slugs pierced it. The helicopter sluggishly gained another three hundred feet when it sputtered and died completely. The blades stopped, and the helicopter falls from the air like dead weight. It landed in the jungle. It was quiet for a moment, and then the helicopter exploded.

Sergeant Meade turned to his mike, "Jones's down, better send in the fly boys. They have us pinned down here on the east side of the clearing."

Captain Bollinger saw the explosion and remained in the air. He spoke into his mike, "They're on their way. They should be there in two. Recommend taking cover."

Christopher Charles

On the screen in front of Bollinger, two blips appeared. "Let's take it up more!" The quad of four helicopters and the two who made it off the ground moved up to two thousand feet as the jets roared in below them.

The jets came in low toward the clearing with their cannons working. Hot lead pierced the jungle coverage below. When they reached the edge of the jungle, the jets dropped four firebombs taking out the jungle for a hundred yards in front of Meade and his men.

Meade slowly stood against the backdrop of flames. He brought the mike to his mouth, "You can bring in Medevac. The clearing's secured." He turned to his men who were slowly standing, "Let's clean it out and start the counting." Meade led his men towards the dying embers in front of him.

Lucky Seven

2 Graduation

James Baughman, medium built, rode his Harley motorcycle through a residential street in upper Pasadena. The houses were expensive. He felt out of place, but he was on his way to pick up his girlfriend, Crystal Hundly. He was wearing a graduation robe over his normal hippy clothes. He sported a bushy beard and moustache. He had worked his way through Pacific Bible College. This was graduation day and the start of a new life for him. He met Crystal the last year of school. He had fallen immediately in love with her. They planned on being married within the month, but they have not told her mother.

He knew she did not approve of him and his style of living, but now that he had graduated, maybe things would change. Jesus forgave his past life. He was a new person wanting only to please God. He turned the last corner and gunned the motorcycle to let Crystal know he was coming.

Crystal Hundly was twenty-one years old, blue eyes, with flowing golden hair. She was standing beside a piano singing a religious song.

Her mother, Mrs. Hundly, older woman in her late fifties, was playing the accompaniment on the piano. She was neatly dressed. Her face beamed with pride as her daughter sung. They were in front of Reverend Herman Gottschalk, a big man wearing a black suit. He was sitting in a comfortable chair, smiling approvingly.

The room was well decorated showing the wealth of the family. Crystal was wearing a graduation robe. Her voice was beautiful impressing the Reverend. Crystal had an innocent nature. Her life had not left any scars. Her voice was pure and came from her soul.

In the background a motorcycle roar pierced the room. Crystal stopped singing, "He's here! He's here!" She ran towards the door.

Mrs. Hundly stood and yelled after her, "You could have at least finished your song!"

Lucky Seven

A Harley motorcycle followed the curved driveway and stopped in front of the expensive house. Jim stepped off the motorcycle. He ran his hand over his long hair attempting to straighten it. He reached into the side compartment and pulled out a long stem white lily. He walked to the door and started to ring the doorbell when the door suddenly opened revealing Crystal.

She leaped at him as he caught her in his open arms. She screamed, "Jim! Jim!"

They were squeezing each other when Mrs. Hundly appeared. She looked embarrassed, "Can we get him inside? We have neighbors!"

Jim ignored her and gave Crystal a passionate kiss, and said softly in her ear, "Love you!"

Crystal became embarrassed knowing her mother was watching and pushed him back. She took him by the hand and attempted to lead him inside, saying, "Maybe we should go inside."

Jim looked up at Mrs. Hundly. He felt her dislike for him and immediately said, "Hello, Mrs. Hundly." Than turning to Crystal, "No, I think I'll wait here for you."

Christopher Charles

Mrs. Hundly gave a sign of relief and stepped back inside the house. Crystal followed, but Jim pulled her back and handed her the lily.

Taking it, Crystal said, "Thank you, it's my favorite flower."

"I know."

Crystal stuck the lily in her dress beneath her robe, "I'll wear it next to my heart." She smiled and gave Jim a big kiss on the lips. Pulling back, she turned and yelled over her shoulder, "Give me a second." She disappeared into the house.

Coming into the music room, Crystal ran to the Reverend Gottschalk, gave him a light hug, "I've got to run. Thank you for coming, Reverend Gottschalk." She turned as her mother entered the room holding up the car keys.

Pushing the keys toward Crystal, "Not the motorcycle, Crystal, please take the keys."

Crystal ignored the keys, and gave her mother a hug, "I'll be safe mother. I won't let him go fast." Before her mother could say more, she ran for the door. Crystal yelled over her shoulder, "See you at the Baccalaureate!"

Lucky Seven

When the door slammed close, Mrs. Hundly went to the window. She saw Crystal climbing on the motorcycle behind Jim and tucking her robe in around her. The motorcycle roared off as Mrs. Hundly closed her eyes a moment and murmured a prayer. She turned back to Reverend Gottschalk, "I can never say no to her. Am I a bad mother?"

"No, Mrs. Hundly, you are a mother who loves her daughter."

"They will accept her right out of college?"

"We want her, not him." Reverend Gottschalk said in an even voice.

"She won't go to your church without him. Is there room in your church for another pastor, Reverend?"

"Maybe, it will be up to the board. Of course, it would help if he wore a suit and cut his hair."

Mrs. Hundly shook her head, "I don't know what she sees in him. After her father died last year, he came into the picture. She was very close to her father." She dropped some tears and moved closer to Reverend Gottschalk.

He backed off slightly, "Maybe he's a father image to her. How old did you say he was?"

"Thirty, I think."

"Does he have a family?"

"Crystal says his parents were killed in an auto accident. He's lived with one relative after another since then. None apparently wanted him for long." She moved closer to the Reverend.

This time the Reverend did not back off allowing her to move into his left arm, "What did he do before entering Bible College?"

"She says he flew helicopters. One of his relatives was a commercial pilot. I don't know if he still has his license."

"At least it's something he can fall back on."

Mrs. Hundly tearfully looked up at the Reverend.

He gave her a hug, "Now don't worry. Things will work out. You must trust God in this. Now, we must hurry if we are going make the Baccalaureate on time."

Lucky Seven

She nodded, and started for door, "Yes, we do not want to miss it."

Jim and Crystal arrived at the college on the motorcycle. They entered the parking lot with Crystal's robe flying out the back. She held on tight as they took a bump. Parking the bike, Crystal hurried towards the building.

The sign outside read:

<table>
<tr><td>PACIFIC BIBLE COLLEGE

BACCALAUREATE 7:00 P.M.</td></tr>
</table>

"Here's where we split," Crystal yelled running towards the open door. "I'll see you after the choir sings. Keep a seat for me." She disappeared into the building.

Jim turned off the machine and calmly walked towards the second door to the auditorium. He noticed Mrs. Hundly and Reverend Gottschalk coming into the parking lot. He ignored them and proceeded into the building. He found two empty chairs in the front row and took them. The auditorium was filling up behind him.

Christopher Charles

When Mrs. Hundly and Reverend Gottschalk entered, the auditorium was almost full forcing them to take a seat near the back.

Minutes later the curtain opened revealing the choir, and Crystal in the front row. She stepped forward and sung the solo portion. Her voice radiated over the audience. She had Jim in tears. As she finished her song, she saw Jim wipe the last of the tears from his eyes. The audience was moved. They stood giving her a standing ovation.

Mrs. Hundly face was beaming with pride as she clapped her hands.

Reverend Gottschalk was clapping enthusiastically, "We have to have her!"

Mrs. Hundly smiled and pressed herself close to him.

Crystal ran from the platform to Jim. They embraced.

Jim wiped the last of the tears away, and softly said, "Love you, I love you very much!"

Crystal blushed, broke the embrace, took Jim's hand, and led him to her mother.

Lucky Seven

Mrs. Hundly gave Crystal a big hug while Jim looked on. Reverend Gottschalk gave Jim a hard look.

Releasing her hug, Mrs. Hundly said, "You were simply beautiful."

Crystal, stepping back, gave a low bow, "Thank you. Thank you all around." Then she gave Reverend Gottschalk a big hug.

"Yes, my dear, you were sensational," Reverend Gottschalk said stepping back. "Now, we'll all have dinner on me."

Crystal looked back at Jim.

Reverend Gottschalk noticed, "Yes, your friend is invited too."

Mrs. Hundly looked displeased, "I don't think I am up to it. You will have to go without me. You can drop me off at home."

"Then it will be the three of us!" Reverend Gottschalk said.

Crystal turned to her mother, gave her a hug, "You sure?"

Christopher Charles

Mrs. Hundly broke the embrace, "Yes, I'll be quite all right. Please go and have a good time."

Later, the three of them were at the local expensive restaurant. Reverend Gottschalk was sitting across from Crystal and Jim.

Finishing desert Crystal moved closer to Jim, looked up at the reverend, and quietly said, "Jim and I are getting married."

Reverend Gottschalk almost dropped his fork. Recovering, he asked, "Does your mother know?"

"I thought I would tell her after we were married."

Reverend Gottschalk cleared his throat. He looked hard at Jim and then back at Crystal, "You have a great gift my dear. It would be a shame to waste it."

"I only sing for God's glory," Crystal replied, and smiled.

"Yes, I know. That is why our church has asked me to set up an appointment for you. We would like you to consider coming."

"And Jim? I will only come if they take Jim too. We have to be together."

Lucky Seven

"Maybe that can be arranged," Reverend Gottschalk said. Then turning to Jim, he continued, "They will want to hear you preach."

"I can preach God's word. I bet they haven't heard that in a while."

"Yes, but I would advise toning it down a bit the first time. Let them get to know you."

Jim glared at Reverend Gottschalk, "I will preach what God tells me, not what man wants me to say."

"Yes, but let's pray God wants you to you to be appointed to our church. I would suggest getting a haircut, and maybe a shave. I am sure you are a very nice-looking man below all that hair."

"Jesus had long hair," Jim responded. "Would you keep him from speaking in your church?"

"No, of course not!"

Crystal interrupted them, pulling on Jim. "Let's not give Reverend Gottschalk a hard time." She moved closer again and gave Jim a light kiss on the cheek. Pushing herself to the outside of the booth, she continued, "Can you gentlemen excuse me a moment?"

Reverend Gottschalk stood, "Yes, of course."

Jim remained in his seat as Crystal stood and turned, "I'll be back in a moment."

"Yes, there is no hurry," Reverend Gottschalk said, as he took his seat. He watched her leave, and continued, "There goes a pure soul. She only sees the good in people." He turned, faced Jim continuing, "She's so fragile and innocent to the world." He allowed this to register a moment. Then he said, "You know under the right guidance she will do a great work for God."

Jim remained quiet and allowed the Reverend to continue. He felt the pressure building. He knew what was coming.

Reverend Gottschalk increased the volume of his voice, "Her gift must be protected. It can be destroyed so easily."

"I can take care of her," Jim said quietly.

Reverend Gottschalk leaned across the table, looked hard at Jim, "Who are you, James Baughman?"

Lucky Seven

"So, I've had a hard life, but God has straightened me out."

It's more than that! Are you ready for responsibility?"

"I can take care of myself."

"What about her?"

"We won't be living off her mother if that's what you're thinking."

"Look at you!" Reverend Gottschalk said increasing the volume of his voice, "You shout rebellion through and through! You're thirty years old, Jim."

"I said I can take care of her!"

"If she loses her innocence, she will lose the voice God has given her. It comes from the heart. She sings what she feels."

"You think I will take this away from her."

"Your life will always be one of contrast. How long do you think she could survive in a world you would provide? You do not even know who you are. When you find out, you will have destroyed her."

Jim started to respond when Crystal returned.

"Did you miss me?"

"Of course, my dear, the world would miss you indeed," Reverend Gottschalk said looking intently at Jim. Standing, he said, "It is time I was leaving. I will see you Sunday at nine sharp."

Crystal, wanting confirmation, "The two of us?"

Reverend Gottschalk smiled, "Of course the two of you. You two will do the service. We will talk afterward."

"I can choose my sermon topic?" Jim asked.

"Certainly, but remember these are people well read in the word," Reverend Gottschalk said.

"You mean comfortable Christians!"

"Look, young man, it is they who will be hiring you. I would suggest pleasing them." Reverend Gottschalk looked at Crystal, and continued, "You better talk to him. Now, I must leave. Thank you for a wonderful evening."

Lucky Seven

Crystal gave Gottschalk a hug and whispered in his ear, "Thank you for dinner. He'll do fine. You will see. He's very good."

"Yes, of course, my dear," Reverend Gottschalk said. He released the embrace, nodded to Jim and left.

Crystal slid in next to Jim, smiled, "He will help us."

"You mean 'you,' he doesn't like me."

"Don't be silly. He just doesn't know you like I do."

Jim took a hug from Crystal, stared out the window a moment, and then he asked, "Do you think I'm good for you?"

"Of course, silly, we're getting married."

Jim pushed Crystal back, held her at arm's length, "Look at me. I don't know who I am."

"You're the man I love."

She started to move closer, but Jim pulled back and shook his head.

Christopher Charles

"Reverend Gottschalk's right. I need to find out who I am."

Crystal sat up, "Reverend Gottschalk! What did he say?"

Jim shook his head, "Nothing, I'm just not sure what God wants me to do."

"He wants you to be with me."

Jim pulled her close, and softly said, "Yes, that part I am sure of."

Crystal remained in his arms, "We'll do the service Sunday. Reverend Gottschalk will make the board like you, and we will be together."

3 Decisions

After dropping Crystal off at home, Jim drove back to his apartment. He could not stop thinking: what did God want him to do? He laid back on his bed and flipped on the T.V.

The news station was showing scenes of the two helicopters exploding in midair and falling to the ground.

The news commentator was describing the scene:

"Two helicopters exploded in a Vietcong ambush killing four American pilots."

There was a brief glimpse of Sergeant Meade's charge.

Christopher Charles

"The soldiers stranded on the ground took heavy losses until two Air Force Jets stopped the charging horde."

Two airplanes flew low over the field of Lilies and dropped their firebombs. The resulting fire consumed the jungle.

"The army said the Vietcong dead body count was good numbering more than a hundred."

Jim shook his head and turned off the T.V. He left a small light on and laid back on his pillow. He was asleep in moments and drifted into a dream state.

Dream:

Jim is driving a jeep over a dirt road leading to a small village of houses and shacks. A large military truck comes up fast behind him and forces his Jeep off the road.

A nine-year old Vietnamese boy is standing in the middle of the road. The boy stares at the oncoming truck unable to move. The truck strikes the boy sending him flying to the right. The truck races on down the road.

Lucky Seven

> Jim finds himself walking through the crowd of angry Vietnamese Villagers, and goes to his knees beside the boy. He lifts the boy to his chest and looks up into the sky. He hears himself praying, "Jesus! Jesus!"

Suddenly everything went blank. He woke up to find himself sitting up in bed with sweat pouring off his body. His mind registered: "Vietnam! God wants me to go to Vietnam!"

The next day he was on his motorcycle looking for the army recruiting office. He found it, parked his bike, and entered the office.

The army recruiter behind the desk looked up at Jim entering the office wearing his hippy clothes and sporting a heavy beard and moustache. He smiled to himself, and asked, "What can I help you with today?"

"I thought I would see what the army has to offer?"

"We can give you a career and training in your field of choice. What are you interested in?"

Jim sat down, looked intently at the recruiter, "Helping people find Jesus. I have a bachelor's degree in ministry."

The recruiting officer cleared his throat, squirmed, "The army is not a Sunday school."

"That's not what I am looking for. I want to help people who really need help and that's Vietnam."

"I don't know, we have plenty of chaplains if that ..."

"No, I don't want to be restricted. I prefer to follow God's lead when I do his work."

"I am not sure what you want?" The recruiter said in a puzzled voice.

"I fly helicopters."

The recruiter's eyes lit up. He leaned forward, "Now we're getting somewhere. Yes, we can put you in one with no problem."

"I don't want to kill people."

The recruiter thought a moment, and then said, "You would be ideal for Medevac. They fly in and pick up the wounded, but they're not taking new recruits right now. Maybe in six months or so, you could try for a position."

Lucky Seven

"I can't wait six months. I think God wants me to go now."

"You could join the army as a helicopter pilot and then transfer to the Medevac unit when a position opens up."

"I said I don't want to kill people."

"We could put that in your contract," the recruiter said.

"You could do that?"

"Yes, but you will have to lose the beard and hair."

"That's okay, I was about to lose it anyway."

Christopher Charles

5 Church Service

Sunday morning in the Presbyterian Church Crystal was singing in front of the choir. The speaker chair beside Reverend Gottschalk on the platform remained empty. The church was less than a third full of conservative dressed senior citizens who sat from the middle to the back of the church.

Crystal looked to her left and caught Gottschalk's eye. He shook his head. She turned and continued to sing, but her face took on a worried look. Then outside the loud sound of a motorcycle coming into the parking lot was heard. She turned and smiled at Gottschalk.

He raised his arms into the air, shook his head, "What did you expect?"

Lucky Seven

Jim entered the choir room and slipped a choir robe over his clothes. He entered the platform clean shaven and his head sporting a military haircut. He took the chair next to Gottschalk.

Crystal smiled, finished her song, and took her seat.

Reverend Gottschalk stood, walked to the pulpit, looked out over the audience, "I would like to introduce our speaker. He is a graduate of Pacific Bible College, an excellent speaker with an interesting point of view." He turned to Jim, continuing, "I present Reverend James Baughman."

Jim stood, came to the pulpit and shook Gottschalk's hand.

Gottschalk nodded and returned to his seat.

Jim stood in front of the pulpit and looked at the audience a moment. Then he said: "You have a very nice church here. The pews are comfortable. The decor is first rate, but you lack one important element, people! Where are your young people? Look around you. Do you see anyone under fifty?"

Christopher Charles

He paused a moment, then continued.

"Most of you will be dead in twenty years, but your church is already dead. Ask yourself how many souls have been saved here say in the last year?"

He paused a moment.

"That's why you have a church. Yes, it's nice to have a senior citizens center, but you need new life. Jesus is life! You need to bring Jesus back to your church."

The congregation begins to squirm in their pews.

"It can be done," Jim shouted. He turned his back to the congregation and faced the choir. Then he RIPPED off his choir robe revealing a large Jesus T-shirt. He turned and revealed the same in front.

Gottschalk and the congregation were in shock.

Jim held up the ripped robe shouting, "Get rid of these!" He allowed this to sit a second, then he continued, "You need music that moves. Then go bring in the young people. Set up a program for young families. You need to make it fun to be here. Then God forbid you should tell someone about Jesus."

Reverend Gottschalk was glaring at Jim.

Jim continued, "When was the last time you told anyone Jesus is alive and well?"

Gottschalk stood, moved behind Jim, and whispered, "I think you need to close now!"

"But I am not finished!"

"Yes, you are!" Gottschalk said, moving Jim aside, taking the pulpit. Then to the congregation, "Those were inspiring words from our new graduate. Something we can all take home. Now let's give him a good hand." He clapped politely, and the congregation followed.

Later in the Clergy room, Jim and Crystal sat together on a bench next to the door.

Crystal faced him and ran her hand over his short hair and clean face, "You were so good. I'm so proud of you. Did I tell you how handsome you look?"

Jim pulled his head back, "I don't think they appreciated it that much. I know Reverend Gottschalk didn't."

"You told them the truth,"

Crystal was about to say more when Reverend Gottschalk entered the room. Jim stood as Crystal ran to Gottschalk and hugged him.

Gottschalk gently pushed her back, faced Jim, cleared his throat, "They want Crystal, but I don't think they're quite ready for you."

"I told you!" Jim responded.

"No, I told you, but you wouldn't listen. You had to do it your way. Well, your way didn't sell. I tried my best."

Crystal glared at Gottschalk, "If they don't want Jim, then they're not getting me. I told you we go together."

Gottschalk looked at Jim and then at Crystal, "You have such a great talent. To see it wasted is a shame. You could do so much for God."

Jim nodded to Gottschalk, "Give us a minute."

Lucky Seven

Gottschalk nodded, left the room, but he remained close enough to hear.

Crystal turned to Jim, "I'm not taking the job. Not without you!"

Jim remained quiet a moment, then he said, "He's right you know. They're not ready for me, and I'm not ready for them."

"I don't know what you mean."

"You're ready to start your career. I'm not. God is still molding me."

"Can't he mold you here with me?"

"They don't want me. That means God doesn't want me here yet."

Crystal was trying to hold back her tears, "Then where does God want you?"

"Vietnam!"

"Oh, dear God, not Vietnam!" Crystal ran to him with her tears flowing, held him close, "You didn't mean it. Say, you didn't mean it!"

Jim caressed her hair tenderly, "Sorry, I've already enlisted."

Christopher Charles

"Tell them you've changed your mind."

"I can't. It's God's will. I feel it deep inside."

"But, we were going to get married."

"We will when I get back. I need to work this through."

Gottschalk entered with a smile on his face, "What have we decided?"

Crystal stepped back from Jim with her tears flowing, "He's going to Vietnam!"

Gottschalk acted shock, "I am sorry you didn't make it here, but Vietnam?"

"It's where God wants me."

"They certainly need chaplains there," Gottschalk said.

"I'll be flying a helicopter," Jim said. "They said I can transfer to a Medevac unit."

Crystal ran back into Jim's arms, "God can't ask that of you."

Lucky Seven

"Wounded men need God the most," Jim said holding Crystal tight. He turned to Gottschalk, "You will take care of her until I come back."

"Of course, I will see to it no harm comes to her."

Crystal cried in Jim's arms.

5 The Military

Jim went through basic training and officer's school. He came out a lieutenant. They transferred him to an airbase in Vietnam. When he stepped off the plane with his duffle bag, he looked around at the temporary buildings on one side of the airfield. Men and machinery continued to move about. Dressed in his military uniform. He watched a quad of helicopters land on one of the pads before he entered the temporary hut marked: CAPTAIN BOLLINGER.

Corporal Matthews, a short, thin young man wearing glasses, was sitting at his desk on the right typing. There was a row of chairs on the left side lining the wall.

A Chuck Grabowsky with his duffle bag at his feet was sitting in the chair opposite Matthew's

Lucky Seven

desk. He was medium built, light hair, strong in the shoulders, and wearing a lieutenant's uniform.

Straight ahead was a door with Captain Bollinger's name on it.

Jim dropped his duffle bag to floor in front of Matthew's desk, and handed him his orders.

Matthew took the orders, and nodded towards Chuck Grabowsky, "Over there, Captain Bollinger will see you both in a minute."

Jim sat next to Chuck and dropped his bag to the floor.

Chuck turned, extended his hand, "Hi, Chuck Grabowsky, I'm somebody's co-pilot."

Jim took his hand, "Could be me, Jim Baughman. I applied for Medevac."

"I heard they have the lowest survival rate here."

Our chances are better. God flies with us.

"God?" Chuck asked.

Christopher Charles

"Flying Medevac helicopters is what God wants me to do. It is his will. I will have his guiding hand."

"God is going to keep bullets from finding your body?" Chuck asked.

"While I am in his grace nothing will happen to me."

"If you go out of grace?"

"That's not very smart knowing the statistics, is it?"

"How about your co-pilot?" Chuck asked.

"I'm sure his grace would extend to you."

"Thanks, I think."

The intercom Buzzed. Corporal Matthew pointed towards Captain Bollinger's door, "You two can go in now."

Jim and Chuck stood with their bags and walked toward the door.

Captain Bollinger, dark hair medium built man, on the other side of the door appeared tired and haggard. He took a sip of his coffee, and slowly shifted through the papers in front of him. He looked up when Jim and Chuck entered and saluted.

"Lieutenant James Baughman reporting for duty, sir," Jim said.

Chuck continued to stand and face Bollinger a few seconds until Bollinger asked, "And you!"

"A....Chuck Grabowsky reporting, sir."

Bollinger waved for them to sit in the two chairs in front of him while he looked at their files.

"Let's see here, yes, here it is." He looked at Chuck, "You have a night problem?"

"I can't fly at night is all. The shadows sort of blurs everything out."

He turned to Jim, "And you're some religious nut on a mission for God." He shook his head, and continued, "Gees, I need pilots, and this is what they send."

Turning back, Bollinger looked at Jim intently, "This is no Sunday school. You will not be interfering with the function of this base."

"No sir, that's not my intent.'

Christopher Charles

"What is your intent?"

"I will wait for God's guidance."

"And what is that?"

Jim shrugged his shoulders, "I don't know."

"Then while you are waiting you will fly helicopters. When you receive your dispensation from God, you will tell me about it before you do it. Is that understood?"

"Yes sir!"

Bollinger turned to Chuck, "And you're not flying unless there's a problem with Baughman here. Your flying report was not all that great even in the daylight. You got that? I'll not be having the lives of my men put at risk by you two. You both got that?"

"Yes sir!" They both said.

"Any questions?"

"When am I going to join the Medevac unit?" Jim asked

Lucky Seven

"Medevac? You signed up for the army helicopter duty. That means you fly the army's helicopters."

"They said I could transfer over to the Medevac unit once I joined the army."

"That's a new unit starting up," Bollinger said. "There's no opening in that unit yet. Didn't they tell you that?"

"Yes sir, but I don't want to kill people," Jim said.

"You don't want to kill people?" Bollinger yelled. "This is war. This is what we do!"

"My contract says I do not kill people," Jim said.

Bollinger looked at Jim's orders again, and saw the line stating he was not required to kill people. He becomes irritated, "You will still fly helicopters mister. You signed up for that, but you will do it without cannon. You'll take Jones's place. He didn't like killing people either, but he didn't have it in writing." Looking up, he asked, "Anymore questions?"

Christopher Charles

"Only one sir, what did Jones do?" Chuck asked.

"He flew into the battle zone and took out the wounded," Bollinger said. "Any more questions?"

Jim and Chuck shook their heads.

"Good, you'll have the morning to get yourself situated. At fourteen hundred hours Sergeant Meade will give you your jungle orientation. I would recommend listening close to what that man has to say. Now, get out of here. Corporal Matthews will show you to your quarters."

Jim and Chuck stood and saluted.

Twenty minutes later Jim and Chuck were entering the officer's quarters. Lockers separated every other bed.

Matthew, clipboard in hand, entered behind Jim and Chuck, "This will be your quarters for the next eighteen months or until we have to move the base again."

"Where is everyone?" Jim asked.

"They have been sent home," Corporal Matthew said. "We'll be filling it up again. You two can have Jones's locker, number seven." He

Lucky Seven

walked to the locker and pulled the name 'Jones' off.

"Number seven wasn't very lucky for him," Chuck said, "How did he take it?"

"He took a hit and crashed in the jungle," Matthew said, "He never knew what hit him. His fuel tank exploded."

"Gee's what's the percentage in here?" Chuck asked.

"No one in here has made it the full term," Matthew said placing Jim's and Chuck's name on the locker. "They either go home maimed or leave in a bag. Jones was the last one in this building. He almost made it."

"Not very cheerful are you," Chuck said.

"No sense in giving you any false hopes," Matthew said.

"We put our trust in God. He does not give false hope," Jim responded.

"Yeah, whatever works for you," Matthew said. "You'll have one jeep between you, but no driver. Yours the one outside marked seven." He placed the number seven on the orders. He

Christopher Charles

handed the paperwork to Chuck, "Here, and good luck."

Matthew walked to the door to leave, but stopped and turned, "You have four hours. That'll give you time for a ride into the village, but you need to be back by fourteen hundred hours. Sergeant Meade will meet you here to show you your helicopter."

"Thanks, but what is the real reason we are in this empty barracks?" Jim asked,

"Gees look at your orders," Matthew said. "The Captain doesn't want you contaminating the other men. Jones was a problem. You see where it got him."

"Thank you for being honest," Jim said.

Matthew nodded and left.

Jim threw his bag on the bed as Chuck hung his up in the locker.

Jim walked over to the window, looked out, "I think we should go into the village."

"Okay, but how did you get them to put that no killing clause in your contract?" Chuck asked.

"I think they needed helicopter pilots, but it may cause us some serious problems. We will have to put our trust in God."

Later:

The jeep was moving along a dirt road with jungle on both sides. The village was just ahead. Chuck was driving. The Jeep was hitting the ruts hard causing Jim to be banged back and forth.

"Slow this thing down!" Jim yelled. "Let's not tempt God!"

Chuck pulled off the road, stopped the jeep, looked hard at Jim, "Lighten up! Gees, this is going to be a long war. I can take this God thing of yours, but you've got to lighten up."

"Sorry, I've just left the most beautiful girl in the world to come here, but God has not shown me why. I know it's not to fly helicopters."

"That's why I'm here. I've wanted to fly all my life. They took away my license in the states. My night problem, you know. My life is flying. There's nothing else. This is the only place I can fly."

"You're lucky," Jim said. "I don't know what my thing is."

Christopher Charles

"Maybe you shouldn't be in all that much of a hurry to find out," Chuck said and started the jeep moving again.

They were coming into the small village of houses and shacks. Kids were playing in the street running back and forth. A village marketplace extended off to the right. As they approached the village, a large military truck came up fast behind them stirring up dust. It forced the jeep off the road and sprayed Jim and Chuck with dirt.

The man on the right side of the truck stuck his hand out the window and showed his contempt for them.

Chuck yelled after them, "Slow down! You're going to kill someone!"

"They're going to hit a kid," Jim said.

The truck roared on into the village. Taylor, a thin nine-year old Vietnamese boy, stood in the middle of the road. The sight of the incoming truck left him powerless to move. The truck struck his body sending him flying to the right side of the road.

Lucky Seven

The villagers came out on the road shouting and waving their fist at the disappearing truck racing on down the road.

Chuck turned to Jim, "How did you know that?"

"It was in my dream. We've got to help that boy."

"We're not doctors! What can we do? We can't even speak the language unless you have been holding out on me."

"Just get going!"

Chuck started the jeep moving slowly until he reached the edge of the village. He kept the motor running, "This is as far as I go. If they start coming after us, I'm out of here."

Jim jumped from the jeep and ran towards the helpless boy.

"Where are you going?" Chuck yelled. "You can't help that kid. You're going to get your head bashed in."

The villagers, holding their threatening broom and rakes in hand, moved aside to allow Jim to

Christopher Charles

reach Taylor. Their angry voices ceased when Jim knelt down beside Taylor.

"Oh God, is this what you wanted me to do?" Jim asked, "Am I supposed to heal this boy?"

An Old Woman came out from the house beside the road banishing her broom, yelling, "Him dead! Him dead! Your truck kill him!"

She began beating Jim until she saw he was not moving from his kneeling position. She moved quietly back into the crowd.

Jim continued to pray, "God, if he's already dead, it's too late." In a trance-like state, Jim lifted Taylor's body to him. Jim's tears flowed. He rocked Taylor back and forth, "Jesus, Jesus heal this boy. Bring him back to life. I feel your energy flowing through me. Heal this boy!"

Chuck timidly approached the crowd and peered over the shoulder of an old man as Taylor's eyes opened.

Taylor looked up at Jim, smiled.

Jim hugged him, "Thank you Jesus! Thank you!"

Lucky Seven

Chuck finally managed to reach Jim, "What did you just do?"

Jim looked up, "Jesus healed him and brought him back to life, Chuck."

Some of the village people clapped while others ran back to their houses.

Chuck looked around suspiciously, "Where's everyone going?"

The old woman looked up at Chuck, "The war make many sick and wounded."

"Are you the boy's mother," Chuck asked.

"Me? I'm old woman. The boy has none. Mother's family die in war. Father's name Taylor, go back home. No one wants boy. Him yours now. "

"What do you mean, ours?" Chuck asked.

"Taylor boy die to save all trouble," the Old Woman said, "You make him live, now him yours."

Chuck pushed his way towards Jim standing with Taylor, but the crowd kept him from reaching him. Finally, he shouted, "Jim, you hear that? They're making this kid ours."

Jim's face was glowing, his tears flowed, he yelled, "I found it, Chuck. I found what God wanted me to do here."

The villagers returned bringing their sick and wounded. They pushed Chuck away.

Chuck pushed back, "What's going on here? What are they trying to do?"

"They don't want you to take him away yet," The Old Woman said.

"Let them be Chuck," Jim said, "This is what God wants."

"You can't heal them all. Let's get out of here while they're still in a good mood."

"You want to take away our miracle?" The Old Woman asked.

The crowd turned towards Chuck. He backed away.

"Me? No, it's okay, but it may not work for all of you. You know, the kid just got hurt."

Lucky Seven

"Don't worry, Chuck. Jesus is here. Can't you feel him?

Chuck looked around, "No, I don't see anyone."

"I can feel him in me."

A man carrying a weak woman pushed into Jim. She gave a feeble hacking cough. Jim looked down and then at Chuck. His eyes said he had to try.

Chuck looked at his watch, "Okay, one hour before we have to leave."

Jim beamed back and placed his hands on the woman. "Jesus! Jesus! You healed once today. Here's one more. Heal her! Heal her of this disease consuming her body."

The weak woman jerked in the man's arms. Slowly she raised her head and tried to cough. Nothing happened. A big smile came to her face. She hugged the man carrying her. He lowered her to the ground.

The woman tugged at Taylor, and said in Vietnamese, "Tell him I feel his magic. Thank him for healing me."

Christopher Charles

Taylor turned to Jim, "She say magic powerful. She thank you."

"Tell her it was Jesus healing her."

Taylor turned to the young woman, and said in Vietnamese, "Jesus heal you. It's not his magic."

The young woman, in Vietnamese, said, "No soldier man heal me. I feel his magic."

Taylor turned back to Jim, "She don't believe you."

The young woman bowed low and backed away to allow others to reach Jim.

"Fine, now you are a god or something," Chuck said.

Jim touched Taylor, "Tell them it's Jesus's magic working through me."

"Who Jesus?" Taylor asked.

Jim pointed to the sky, "God!"

Taylor pointed to the sky, "God!"

Lucky Seven

A man on a wooden crutch pushed his way into Jim.

"No, you don't understand," Jim said.

"Man wants magic," Taylor said.

"But you know who Jesus is?

The man pushed into Jim again.

"Man wants magic not Jesus," Taylor said.

"Maybe you should heal them first and tell them who Jesus is later," Chuck said.

Jim looked at the crowd expecting him to heal them. A young girl with a bleeding leg looked up at him. "Okay, tell them it's Jesus healing them whether they believe it or not."

"Then you heal them?" Taylor asked.

"Then Jesus will heal them," Jim replied.

Taylor turned to the crowd. His face broke out in a big smile. In Vietnamese, he said, "His name Jesus. He heal all of you."

The crowd murmured their approval and pushed in closer.

Jim smiled, held the girl's leg, and prayed, "I feel your energy coming back inside of me, Jesus. It's building. Jesus heal this wound. Heal this little girl for your glory."

He wiped off her bloody leg revealing a normal leg. The Old Woman handed him a cloth to wipe his hands while the crowd gasped in amazement and swayed back and forth in a spiritual trance.

The girl hugged Jim and ran to her mother. The mother cried.

Later:

A man laid on his stomach revealing a large wound on his back. Jim, tired and haggard, went to his knees, took the wound, and squeezed it together.

Chuck paced back and forth behind Jim, yelling, "This is it. No more. The man can take no more. Tell them Taylor."

Jim's voice was hoarse, "Heal him Jesus. Heal him."

Lucky Seven

Jim rubbed his hand back across the wound revealing smooth skin. He wiped his bloody hands in the towel.

Chuck helped Jim to stand, "Tell them Taylor. Tell them he can't do it anymore."

"I can't stop now. There's more."

"There's another day," Chuck said, "You're a mess." We've got to fly in forty minutes."

The Old Woman handed Jim a bowl of local brew, "Here, take this. It make you feel top notch."

Chuck pushed the bowl back, but some of it spilled on Jim's clothes. "Take this stuff away. That would be all he needs. We're heading out."

"I make it myself. Look what it do for me," the Old Woman said. She lifted her dress slightly and danced around Jim and Chuck.

Chuck, ignoring her, lifted and dragged Jim towards the Jeep.

Taylor turned to the crowd behind them, and said in Vietnamese, "Jesus needs to rest now. He come back later."

Christopher Charles

Taylor ran back to Chuck who placed Jim in the Jeep. Taylor lifted Jim's legs in and climbed in behind him.

"Easy there Taylor," Chuck said.

"I go with Jesus."

"He has to fly. You will have to stay here."

"Jesus go heal soldiers now?" Taylor asked

"Something like that, now out of the there. We'll be back for you later."

Taylor reluctantly climbed out of the jeep, "You promise to bring Jesus back?"

"He's not Jesus. He's Lieutenant Baughman.

Taylor ran to Jim and hugged him tight, "Promise you bring back Jesus?"

Jim's voice was hoarse. "I'll be back, Taylor. We have to go."

Taylor released Jim slowly, stepped back, "You promise Taylor."

"We'll be back."

Lucky Seven

Chuck stepped in the driver's side of the Jeep, started it, and left Taylor in the dust.

Taylor, watching the Jeep drive off, wiped a tear, "Jesus come back. He promised. Not like Taylor dad."

Chuck, driving the jeep back over the dirt road glanced at the semi-conscious Jim drifting back and forth with the jeep's movement. "You going to be able to fly?"

"You fly it. I'll ride along this time," Jim mumbled.

"Yeah, that might be a good idea."

Jim closed his eyes allowing himself to drift off.

"How did you do that back there?" Chuck asked.

"I didn't do it. Jesus did," Jim replied in a hoarse voice.

"That's good for them. Now, how did you really do it?"

"I'm not sure exactly. I felt this strange energy come over me. When I touched them, the energy left me and went into them. You saw what happened."

"Yeah, I saw alright. You scared the hell out of me. What happens when you touch someone not sick?"

"I don't know? Nothing I think. The energy's gone now. Everything is gone. I've got nothing left."

"You have to hang in there until after our flight."

Jim nodded and dosed off.

Chuck looked over, "Yeah, like that's going to work."

6 Recon. Flight

The jeep entered the base and pulled into the spot marked seven next to the building. Meade, in his jeep, was already there staring at them.

"I think we're a little late," Chuck said as he gave Jim's sleeping body a hard shake. "Time to wake up. Our guide is here."

"Who? Tell him we'll do it tomorrow."

Meade climbed out of his jeep and walked towards Jim and Chuck.

"I don't think he's going to buy that."

Christopher Charles

Meade nodded to Chuck as he approached their jeep. "Say you didn't go to the village and try some of their local brew."

"We went to the village, but he didn't touch a drop."

Meade leaned over, smelled Jim, "Yeah right. He's the preacher?"

Chuck nodded, "You're Sergeant Meade?"

Sergeant Meade nodded, and looked up, "You okay?"

"I feel fine."

Meade climbed into the back of the jeep, "Then let's go."

Chuck turned around in the jeep, and asked, "What happened to 'Sir'?"

"When you ninety-day wonders earn it, I'll call you, sir."

"They put us through ninety days of boot camp. We earned it."

"Not out here you haven't. Jones thought he was a hot shot officer. He didn't meet the test."

Lucky Seven

"What test?"

"I heard you can fly. Let's go see."

Chuck pressed the accelerator. The Jeep jerked and raced away from the building. A few minutes later the jeep pulled up to pad #3. A helicopter with no cannon or missiles sat on the pad with a number 7 painted on the side.

Meade climbed out of the jeep.

Chuck stepped out and made a tour around the #7 helicopter.

Jim slowly walked over to the helicopter, bowed his head, and prayed.

Chuck worked his way to the other side of the helicopter. He looked back at Meade, "I've never flown one of these."

"What do you mean? They had you fly in your ninety-day wonder school."

"Only simulators, but they can't be that hard." Chuck came around the helicopter, and ignored Jim standing with his head bowed.

"What's wrong with him?" Sergeant Meade asked.

Christopher Charles

"I think he's praying. I wouldn't disturb him if I were you."

Chuck climbed into the helicopter.

Meade watched Jim, "How long is he going to take?"

"When he's ready, he'll get in. Are you coming?"

"Yeah, sure," Meade said, and climbed into the helicopter behind Chuck.

Inside the helicopter Chuck found the co-pilot's seat. Meade sat in a jump seat behind the pilot seat. It faced back towards the interior of the helicopter. The large evacuation door was beside him.

Chuck strapped himself in, looked the controls over, "It looks like the simulator." He shook the control bar, "I wonder what this is for?

Sergeant Meade placed his helmet, turned around, "They said you flunked night flying. Can our religious nut fly any better?"

"Then you should feel safe. It's light outside. My hair doesn't get long until after dark, then I can't see."

Lucky Seven

Jim worked his way into the helicopter and took the pilot's seat. He slipped his helmet on, whirled his finger upward, "Let's go!"

"How you feeling?" Chuck asked.

"Better."

Chuck donned his helmet, adjusted his mike, pushed the start button, and the rotors came alive. The helicopter wobbled slightly and then lifted off the pad.

Sergeant Meade stood and turned towards the cockpit to see out the windscreen. He braced himself between the pilot and co-pilot seat. Chuck spoke into his helmet mike. "I've never flown one this big before."

Meade tightened his grip on the handhold, and into his helmet mike, he said, "Just take us straight out."

"Aye, aye, Sergeant," Chuck said.

The helicopter skimmed over the trees.

Meade leaned forward, looked out the windscreen, "You can take us higher."

Christopher Charles

Chuck looked the controls over. "Let's see... What does that?" He fiddled with the controls. It took the helicopter up. "There! Gees, this is fun."

Meade, ignoring him, pointed to the canyon ahead, "Go through that pass. We've been operating on the other side of it."

The helicopter moved rapidly up the steep pass remaining low.

"How high is this pass?" Chuck asked.

"A lot higher than this. Take this thing up."

"Let's see, how did I do that? Aw, here." Chuck pulled the flight stick back slightly.

The #7 helicopter skimmed the trees, barely missed a protruding rock, and headed straight for the canyon wall.

Meade shouted into his mike, "Dammit, Grabowsky! Quit showing off! Turn this craft."

"I didn't hear sir."

"Turn the dam craft, sir. Now!"

"Anything you say."

Lucky Seven

The helicopter banked right and just missed the steep canyon wall and came out on top of the pass.

Chuck spoke into his helmet mike, "Jim, you feel like flying?"

Speaking into his helmet mike, Jim said, "I'm feeling better."

"I thought he was drunk?" Meade asked.

"I feel better since I prayed. I can take it now, Chuck."

"I'm writing this up when we get back," Sergeant Meade said.

"Now that's positive thinking," Chuck said.

The helicopter left the pass, and then dropped down over the jungle. It remained twenty feet above the trees and continued to move fast.

Meade relaxed, said, "Okay, you can fly, now take her up, sir."

"Yes Sergeant, taking her up," Jim said.

Christopher Charles

The helicopter swung up to a thousand feet. In the jungle an open area the size of a three-football fields appeared.

Meade leaned forward, "That's a staging area we use. It's the only clear area around. Lieutenant Jones bought it here, another wise-guy."

"You don't like air jockeys?" Chuck asked.

"I don't like ones who jeopardizes my men who have to fly with them."

"What's that white stuff all over the field?" Jim asked.

"Flowers," Meade said. "It's called the field of lilies by the natives. Somebody cleared the jungle and planted them."

"You don't say..." Jim took the craft lower.

"What are you doing?" Meade asked.

"Just checking it out for the best approach."

"We haven't been here for a while," Meade said, "Could be VC."

The helicopter took a power dive, came in low over the jungle, and dropped into the field. It remained ten feet hovering over the surface facing the far side of the field.

Jim looked out the windscreen at the field of blooming lilies, "I need to come back here and take a picture."

Suddenly gunfire erupted around them. Looking out the windscreen, they saw three missiles coming straight for them.

The helicopter dropped a foot as two missiles pass beneath the rotors. The third one remained on course. The helicopter tipped to the left. The third missile passed the door and rocked the helicopter slightly.

Meade watched the missile go pass the open door, and yelled, "Let's get the hell out of here!"

Jim took the helicopter up quickly and moved it back over the jungle.

Meade turned around and sat back in his seat, "You're one of the luckiest pilots I've ever seen, or you're that good."

"Sometimes a little prayer goes a long-ways," Jim said.

Christopher Charles

"Maybe number seven is lucky after all," Chuck said.

"If you sirs have had enough, I'm for going home."

"Why thank you Sergeant." Chuck said and nodded to Jim, "Then home it is."

"Maybe you better take her on in," Jim said.

"My pleasure," Chuck said, and took the controls.

Jim listened to the sound of the rotors and drifted off into a dream state. He saw Crystal walking through the field of lilies towards him.

7 Adjustments

Jim and Chuck entered the building marked, 'Captain Bollinger'. They saw Corporal Matthew and started towards him, when he waved them off, "Take a seat over there. He'll be with you in a minute. He's talking to Sergeant Meade."

Jim collapsed in a chair.

Chuck took a seat beside him, and looked up at Mathew, "You get a chance to look at our report?"

"Which one of you is Lucky Seven?" Corporal Matthew asked.

"Who's saying that?" Chuck asked.

"Sergeant Meade for one, it's all over the base."

Christopher Charles

"It was Jesus answering prayer," Jim responded.

"You call it what you want. The Sergeant's calling it luck."

Jim allowed it to slide and collapsed back in his chair.

Matthews continued to type.

Chuck leaned over and whispered to Jim. "What happened out there? I thought we bought it for sure."

Jim straightened himself up and whispered. "I don't know. Everything was in slow motion. I could actually see the bullets and missiles. I just turned to avoid them.

Chuck started to say more when Bollinger's door opened, and Meade crossed the room. Meade gave Jim a hard-evaluating stare before going outside.

"Not much has changed with him," Chuck said.

"You two can go in now," Matthew said.

Lucky Seven

They both stood and walked toward Captain Bollinger's office.

Captain Bollinger was sitting at his desk looking at his clip board. The door opened, Jim and Chuck entered. They started to salute when Bollinger motioned for them to sit down.

"Did Meade have anything good to say?" Chuck asked.

"You got his attention," Captain Bollinger said. He paused and looked Jim straight in the eye, "I expect my men to fly sober. You got that? You lay off that village brew."

"Yes sir!"

He turned to Chuck, "That show-off top gun routine belongs back home to impress the girlfriends not my top sergeant. You got that?"

"Yes sir. I just thought I had to earn his respect."

"You earn it by doing your job. You've both have taken your share of luck on this one. You better stop pressing it. Keep Jones in mind, he thought he was good too."

"How'd he get it?" Chuck asked.

"He flew in before the fire field was secured. His sergeant was Meade."

"I hear he didn't like him much," Chuck said.

"Look, Meade's a good soldier. He doesn't like his pilots taking chances with the lives of his men. You two take this serious, or you're both out of here in a bag or otherwise, any questions?"

"No sir," Chuck replied.

Bollinger looked at Jim, "And you?"

"No sir."

"Then Matthews has your duty roster. 'On-call' means 'On-call'. You're not restricted to the base unless you can't control yourself. That means no booze or women. When your unit goes into action, you go into 'Stand-by'. That means you're restricted to the base. You got that?"

Jim and Chuck nodded.

"Okay, you're out of here."

Jim and Chuck stood and started to salute.

Bollinger waved them off, "We're not all that formal around here. Best you start adjusting."

Lucky Seven

"Yes sir."

Jim and Chuck nodded and left. Going back out to the waiting room, Corporal Matthew handed them schedules and a radio pack.

"These are the days you are on call but leave your radio on in case things change. If we take a big hit, everyone's involved."

"I guess we didn't make many points today," Chuck said.

"I don't know," Corporal Matthew said, "You're getting tomorrow off."

Chuck smiled.

The next day Chuck was driving the jeep towards the village while Jim rode beside him, "I don't think this is such a good idea," Chuck said.

"I promised Taylor I'd come back."

"Can you handle another session like the last one?"

"When they see I am not leaving them, they may not push so hard."

"I think you have something else in mind."

Christopher Charles

"Yes," Jim paused a moment, and continued, "Jesus healed their bodies, now he must save their souls."

"Always a catch."

"Gees, they think I'm Jesus. I've got to change that."

Ahead was the village. Taylor sat by the front door of the Old Woman's house looking down the road. He saw the Jeep, jumped to his feet, and shouted, "Jesus is coming! Jesus is coming!"

The people in the village came out of their houses and filled the dirt road.

Taylor ran up to the Jeep as it stopped. "I knew you come back. I knew it."

Jim stepped out of the Jeep and held up his hand to stop the advancing crowd. Chuck remained behind the wheel.

"Taylor, tell them I just come to visit this time. Jesus will heal them later."

Taylor turned back to the crowd and held up his hands. In Vietnamese he said, "Jesus tired today. He come to see Taylor this time."

Lucky Seven

The crowd murmured loudly. Then they slowly dispersed back to their homes.

The Old Woman came outside. "I heard what you said, Taylor. You tell them right."

Taylor ran back and hugged Jim. "I tell them right. Jesus come back to see Taylor."

"Yes, you told them right. Now we have things to do."

Taylor jumped back from Jim with a big grin on his face, "What do you want Taylor to do?"

Jim looked around. "Where can we build a church?"

"What's church?"

"A place where scared things are taught."

The Old Woman asked, "Why build one? We have one two miles from village. Taylor knows where."

"It might be better to build a new one."

"Why? No one goes there now. It's been empty for many years."

Christopher Charles

"Let's go look at it," Chuck said, "I don't think Jesus would mind."

"Taylor show you where."

"Okay, let's go look." Jim said.

Jim climbed in the Jeep. Taylor jumped in the back seat, smiled, and waved to the few people looking on. In moments the Jeep was moving slowly down a narrow jungle trail. The brushes scraped the sides of the Jeep in places.

"Where is this temple?" Chuck asked. "We're getting too far from the airbase."

"We almost there," Taylor said, "You like, you see."

They came to an old stone roofless temple. It stood in the middle of a small clearing filled with brush and jungle overgrowth. Jim pulled the jeep up to the open doorway. He stepped out of the jeep and walked into the building in a reverent matter. Chuck and Taylor remained in the Jeep.

Inside the temple a stone altar sat at the far end. The roof was gone, but the stone walls remained solid. Jim prayed a moment, and then looked around slowly. Chuck and Taylor entered.

Lucky Seven

"What do you think?" Chuck asked.

"It feels good. I think Jesus approves," Jim said. "We still have to put on a roof."

"I tell village people. They do it, no problem."

"Then we will make this our church."

Taylor ran to Jim, gave him a hug, and looked up at him. Tears filled eyes, "Jesus stay here?"

"Yes, Jesus will stay here."

Taylor buried his head into Jim.

Two days later at the airbase

Military people are moving between the portable buildings. Jim and Chuck were walking fast toward a MASH building.

"Where are we going this morning, Jim me boy?"

"I thought I would check out the MASH unit."

"We can't just go in there. You're not a chaplain."

"But I can heal them. I feel it inside. Why should I only heal the Vietnamese?"

Christopher Charles

"This is not the local village crowd. They're not going to let you walk in there and start healing people. I mean we're helicopter pilots not doctors."

"Jesus wasn't a doctor either, but he healed people."

"I'm not doubting that you can heal them. I've seen you in action, but they haven't."

"Then it's time they did."

Jim and Chuck entered a temporary building with sign over the door that read "MASH UNIT". A desk and filing cabinets occupied one side of the room, and office spaces occupied the other side. The aisle remained open to the waiting surgery rooms ahead. A hallway led off to the recovery room on the right.

Jim and Chuck entered and walked by the desk. A female nurse came out of the surgery room rolling a wounded soldier on a bed. They followed the Nurse at a discreet distance up the hallway. They watched the Nurse roll the bed into the recovery room.

Lucky Seven

A few minutes later the Nurse returned with the empty bed and stopped in front of them, "Is he a friend of yours?"

Jim started to speak when Chuck stepped in front of him. "We wanted to see how he was doing?"

"He's by the worst of it, but the next twenty-four hours are critical."

"Can we see him?"

"He won't know you're there, but you can take a peek at him if it will make you feel better. He could use a good prayer about now."

"Yes, thank you," Jim said.

Jim and Chuck were about to enter the room.

The Nurse stopped, and turned, "I'm not supposed to let anyone near him yet, but since he's your friend maybe just a quick peek. I'll be back in a moment."

"Yes ma'am. Thank you," Chuck said as they moved inside the room.

The Nurse nodded approvingly and moved the bed up the hall.

Christopher Charles

Inside the recovery room were several curtained off areas that extended around the room. All of them were empty except one. Jim and Chuck walked to the occupied bed.

"You sure you want to do this?" Chuck asked.

"The nurse said he needed a prayer. That's all we're going to do."

"You know what I mean. Once you start this, there's no turning back. There's going to be questions asked."

"Not if we hurry. They don't know who we are. Stand by the door and watch for the nurse."

Chuck went back to the door as Jim stepped beside the bed. Tubes stuck out of the man's arm and extended to overhead bottles. The man's head, left ear and arm were in bandages. Jim placed his hand on the bandages and waited.

Chuck whispers from the door. "She's coming back. Do it or forget it."

"I can't until I feel the energy. Stall her. It's coming."

Chuck moved out into the hallway and stepped in front of the approaching Nurse coming down the hall, "Give him a minute. They were very close."

"His head wound was quite severe," the Nurse said. "They don't think he will make it. I hope your friend is prepared for that."

"What are his chances?" Chuck asked.

"He's in God's hands now."

"Then he should be in good hands."

"Excuse me," the Nurse said and pushed Chuck aside. "I have to check on my patient now. That's all the time I can give him."

The Nurse entered the recovery room. She screamed as Jim ran out of the recovery room.

Going past Chuck, he yelled, "Let's go!"

Chuck hesitated until he heard a second scream louder than the first one. He turned and followed Jim up the hallway.

They turned the corner and ran toward the front door as two doctors came out of the operating room. They looked at the fleeing two, but they are drawn to the SCREAMS down the hall.

Christopher Charles

The Nurse leaned against the wall pointing to the recovery room as the two doctors ran past her and disappeared inside.

Jim and Chuck ran between the buildings until they reach their barracks and the jeep. Jim jumped in.

Chuck, coming up behind him, took the passenger seat, and held Jim back from starting the engine, "What happened back there?"

"I took his bandages off."

"You what?"

"He woke up. I wanted to see if he was healed," Jim said. He started the Jeep and backed out.

"And?"

"He was."

"Then why are we running?"

"To avoid trying to explain it."

"The village? It's been two days."

"The best place I know to hide."

Lucky Seven

Jim drove through the village, but no one was around. He looked a Chuck, "Temple!"

Chuck nodded, "Let's go."

As they approached the temple, they saw the new roof of woven grass. The village people moved about the temple as Jim and Chuck arrived in the Jeep.

Taylor ran toward them. "I told them you come back when we finish roof. Good job, right."

Jim stepped from the Jeep, looked around, "Very nice Taylor. Why is everyone here?"

"They wait for Jesus. Some been here two days."

Jim walked inside the temple. It was "wall" to "wall" Vietnamese people with more squeezing inside. They sat or laid on the dirt floor. When Jim and Chuck entered with Taylor, a strong murmur went around the room.

Jim walked with Taylor to the little altar at the far end of the temple. He stood a moment, looked out at the people, then raised his hands, "Please Jesus accept this building as your own. We dedicate it to you and your glory."

Finished, Jim sat on the altar, turned to Taylor beside him, "Okay, bring them up, Taylor."

Taylor walked out into the crowd. He pointed to an old man. Two men lifted and brought the old man forward.

In Vietnamese Taylor said, "Okay, Jesus heals now."

Chuck remained by the door, looked around apprehensively, "Where did all of these people come from, Taylor?"

"Many villages. They all come to Jesus. They know he make them well."

Jim healed the old man as Chuck received a call over the radio.

Chuck spoke into radio, "Yes sir. Right away, sir. We're on our way in." Chuck came up behind Jim and whispered, "We've been caught, time to go back. It was Captain Bollinger."

Jim nodded and motioned to Taylor for one more.

A diseased woman with bad teeth came forward coughing up huge balls of Green Fluid.

Lucky Seven

She spit the fluid on the floor and knelt in front of Jim.

Jim prayed, "Heal her Jesus. Heal this woman for your glory."

The woman stopped coughing, stood, lunged forward, and kissed Jim square on the mouth.

Jim stood wiping his mouth. He turned to Taylor, "Maybe we had better be going. Taylor tell them."

In Vietnamese Taylor said, "See what you did. Now Jesus is going."

Walking towards the door, Jim said, "Taylor, we'll be back first chance we get."

"Do you want me to hold people here?"

"No, I am not sure when they will let us come back," Jim said climbing into the Jeep.

Chuck already had the motor running. As soon as Jim was in, the Jeep leaped forward heading back to the base.

Taylor watched them disappear down the road, and said to himself, "Don't worry Jesus, I keep everyone here."

Christopher Charles

8 Reprisals

Captain Bollinger sat in his office reading a memo from the Mash Unit. He worked his cigar around in his mouth and grunted to himself a few times.

The intercom came alive. Corporal Matthew voice came through, "They're here!"

Captain Bollinger pressed the intercom button, "Send them in!"

Jim entered with Chuck behind him, "Lieutenant Grabowsky and Lieutenant Baughman reporting, sir."

Bollinger motioned for them to sit, stared hard at them, "I hear you've been visiting the Mash Unit."

Christopher Charles

"Yes sir," Jim responded.

"Did anyone tell you to interfere with them?"

"No sir."

"Do you have a license to practice medicine I don't know about?"

"No sir."

"Then stay the hell away from there. You got that mister? If I hear you're there again, I'll have you in the brig. You got that?" Bollinger turned to Chuck continuing, "And you Grabowsky. I gave you more credit. You keep him in line, or you'll be going down with him."

"Yes sir."

Then looking at both of them, he said, "You're on standby. Your unit's going out tonight."

"Night flying, sir?" Chuck asked.

"That's right. Baughman will do the flying. You'll be just riding along."

"Yes sir."

Lucky Seven

"What a freak show you two make. I get one good pilot out of the two of you. Now get out of here!"

Jim and Chuck stood and quickly left. Once they were outside, Chuck gave a big sigh of relief, "I thought we bought it back there."

"The man was healed. I'm sure the patient appreciated that, but it's no more Mash Units."

"I think the Captain made that clear enough," Chuck said.

Later that night four helicopters on Pad #2 were being loaded. Men scrambled aboard taking up their positions.

Sergeant Meade watched, and yelled at the men, "Load! Load! Move it! When I tell you to move, you move it! It could save your life."

On Pad #3 Jim and Chuck watched Meade load his men.

"He's a tough one," Jim said.

"Yeah, we better be checking Lucky Seven out," Chuck said. "I don't want anything going wrong in the dark."

Christopher Charles

Jim held Chuck back, "Let's pray first."

Chuck nodded.

"Jesus protect us on this mission. Help us to glorify your name." Finished, Jim looked up, "Okay, let's go."

"Did you have to put that last part in?"

Jim smiled and leaped into the helicopter.

On Pad #2 the quad of helicopters lifted off.

A few moments later helicopter #7 lifted off and climbed into the night sky. The jungle was dark below. As the helicopter approached the clearing, they could see exploding shells and tracer bullets of a firefight below.

Over their speaker they heard Sergeant Meade's voice, "They were waiting for us. We took eight causalities. We need to evacuate them immediately. The area is secured, setting the flares."

"That's our cue," Jim said, and brought the helicopter in low focusing on the four burning flares that form a rectangle. He came in fast and landed.

Lucky Seven

Looking out the windscreen, he saw shadows of men came up from the grass. They ran for #7 helicopter carrying the wounded men. Bringing them in through the helicopter's wide-open side door, they placed the wounded on the stretchers that hung from bulkhead. They stacked the stretchers four deep on each side of the helicopter to get everyone inside. It was dark. Only a dim yellow light illuminated the men lying on stretchers.

Chuck strapped in the last one and yelled, "Ready back here."

"Then we're out of here." Jim pulled back on the stick taking the helicopter up into the dark night above the jungle as a shell EXPLODED beneath it. The helicopter rocked badly, but it managed to straighten out and fly into the darkness.

Chuck worked his way back to the co-pilot's seat, "No damage inside. How's it handling?"

"Seems to be holding together. Here, takeover.

Where are you going?" Chuck asked.

"Back there."

Christopher Charles

"You know I can't fly at night."

"The heading's set. Just hold her in the air a few minutes."

The speaker came alive, "What's your ETA?"

Chuck looked at Jim and shrugged his shoulders.

"Tell them twenty minutes."

Chuck nodded and talked into his helmet mike.

Jim worked his way between the stretchers. The man on the top hanging stretcher was unconscious. His body and clothes on the left side reeked with blood.

Jim touched him and prayed. "Heal him Jesus. Heal him. Thank you, Jesus, I feel your energy working."

The man opened his eyes and started to raise his head, but Jim eased him back and moved on to the man below him.

In the Cockpit Chuck tried to see out into the darkness, and yelled, "I can't see a thing. You better make it fast."

Lucky Seven

On pad #3 the ambulance and personnel were waiting for the helicopter.

In the helicopter Jim had healed seven of the wounded. He was kneeling down to the man on bottom stretcher.

The man sat up slightly and shouted, "Don't you dare touch me. This is my ticket home. I saw what you did to them. You leave me alone."

"Okay, if you prefer, but Jesus can heal your leg."

The wounded soldier gave Jim a defiant look.

Suddenly the helicopter jerked abruptly.

Chuck yelled, "What's going on back there? I can't hold this thing."

Jim looked up. The healed men were trying to climb out of their hanging stretchers.

"Everyone stay put!" Jim yelled. "Slowly, all of you back into the stretchers."

The men realizing the problem worked their way back into their stretchers as Jim moved forward to the cockpit.

Christopher Charles

"Coming back Chuck, I'm finished here."

"It's about time. They're screaming for us to land, and I can't see the ground."

"Be there in a minute," Jim said working his way between the seats. He took the controls. Below him was the airbase. He saw the #3 pad and the military ambulances standing by. He hovered the helicopter over the pad and brought it down.

When the helicopter was down the ground grew swung into action. People entered the helicopter through the large open door and took out the stretchers with the men on them. The military ambulances backed in, and the men were quickly placed inside.

The wounded soldier with injured leg came out screaming, "Easy with that leg. I'm the only one wounded here. Take it easy."

The ambulances filled up quickly. Their lights flashed as they drove toward the MASH unit.

Jim and Chuck emerged from the helicopter.

"They're going to want to know how you did it."

Lucky Seven

"I didn't, Jesus did."

"That's not going to work, and you know it."

The military ambulances pulled up beside the Mash Unit. The men were removed quickly and brought inside. The doctors began examining the healed men. They cut the blood stain clothes off and looked for the open wounds.

Victor Novak, war correspondent, medium height, slightly balding came in unnoticed. He talked to the only wounded soldier. "They were all wounded you say."

"It was the lieutenant in the helicopter. He came back and healed everyone. Spooky!"

I wouldn't let him touch me"

"Why not?"

"I've got my reasons."

Captain Miller, the head doctor of the Mesh Unit, tall man, dressed in surgical scrubs, noticed Novak, and yelled, "What's he doing here? Get him out of here."

Christopher Charles

Victor Novak spoke quickly to the wounded soldier. "Looks like I've got to go. I'll talk to you later." He quickly ducked out the door.

One hour later in the war room ten officers of various ranks sat around a rectangle table facing the Commanding Officer, Colonel Hardgrove, a hard man with broad shoulders. He started the session by saying, "Let's have your reports on tonight's action gentlemen. Bollinger, you start."

"We went into action in sector 'D' on reports the VC were operating there. It was supposed to be a surprise action, but they were waiting for us."

"Then we have a security problem," Captain Hardgrove said.

"We think the VC are observing our movements locally. There's something going on in the village that's bringing in a lot of outside Vietnamese. Probably the VC are coming in with them."

"Eliminate it, Captain. I'll not have my men shot up because of some local problem."

"Yes sir."

Lucky Seven

"Now that brings us to our second problem," Colonel Hardgrove said. "We have men claiming to be wounded, yet upon inspection there's not a mark on them. Is that correct, Captain Miller?"

Captain Miller cleared his throat, "Yes sir. They had blood on them. At first inspection you would say they were wounded, but they didn't have a bruise."

"Sergeant Meade, can you enlighten us?" Colonel Hardgrove asked.

"Yes sir. The men I sent back were all wounded. I don't know what happened in the transport."

"Captain Bollinger, anything to add?" Colonel Hardgrove asked. "It was your men who transported them."

"I'm looking into it, sir."

"Maybe I can help," Colonel Hardgrove said. "A Victor Novak, a reporter for the Star, says the men were healed by Jesus. Now who is this Jesus?"

Christopher Charles

"It's not Jesus. It's Lieutenant Baughman," Captain Bollinger said, "He's been causing us some problems."

"Did he heal them or not?" Colonel Hardgrove asked.

Bollinger leaned back in his chair, chewed his cigar a few seconds, then said, "It appears he did, sir."

"Then we have a problem," Colonel Hardgrove said. "Do we exploit him or get rid of him?"

"I don't want him hanging around my MASH unit, Captain Miller said. "He's already caused me enough disruption. If he's really healing people, which I don't think he is, I'll lose all control of my staff."

"I think you said it," Colonel Hardgrove said. "To keep him here we face total disruption. We will become a big spectacle for the news media, and this Lieutenant will have taken over my base. We have to move quickly here or end up with egg on our face."

Captain Miller banged the table, shouting, "Send them back to the states. Let the news media have their day with him there, not here. Give these fakers enough rope, they will always hang themselves."

"Captain Bollinger, do you agree?" Colonel Hardgrove asked.

"If it gets him out of my hair, I'm for it."

"Then let's send him, and who's the other one?" Colonel Hardgrove asked.

"Lieutenant Grabowsky, sir," Captain Bollinger said.

"Yes, send him too, place them both on a two-month furlough. That should give us some time to figure a way to handle this. Can you set this up, Bollinger?"

"Yes sir."

Later

Jim was talking to Crystal using Matthew's phone. "Yes, I'm coming home. Not for good, only two months."

Crystal was on the phone in the music room, "You're not hurt or anything?"

Christopher Charles

"No, nothing like that. I've been healing people."

"Healing people?"

"Yes."

"Really? They're sending you home for that?"

"I think it embarrasses them."

"Then what the papers say is true?"

"Yes, I feel Jesus' power in my arms and hands. When I touch people, it heals them."

"Oh Jim, I knew God would give you something special. I love you so much."

Static came on the line.

Colonel Hardgrove was sitting at the table with Matthews in the war room. The lines to the phone go through the equipment in the room. They were listening to the conversation on a speaker.

Over the speaker phone, Jim said, "I love you. I think the line is going."

"Love you..." Crystal replied.

Lucky Seven

Hardgrove nodded to Matthews, "Do it!"

The phone went dead. A recording come on line, "Your time allotment is finished. Try again tomorrow."

"I won't be here tomorrow. Can you try again?"

The line goes dead.

In their quarters Chuck was packing his duffle bag when Jim entered. "Did you get through?"

"For a minute before they cut me off."

"You'll be there in a couple of days."

Jim opened his locker, stopped, and closed it again, 'We've got to go back to the village."

"Bollinger said we're on standby until we leave tomorrow."

Victor Novak entered unnoticed.

"I can't leave Taylor hanging for two months," Jim said. "If we go to the village now, we can be back before dark."

"You don't mind if I tag along?" Victor Novak asked.

Chuck turned quickly, saw Novak, "Who are you?"

"You best friend or your worst enemy, it depends on you. The name's Vic Novak. I'm with the Star."

"There's nothing to see here," Chuck said.

"Look guys, I know what you've been doing. The whole base knows."

"That's why we're going home."

"You're going home because they don't know what to do with you. You've caused them some waves. You're like innocent babes in a den of wolves, and you don't even know it."

Jim walked towards the door, "Let him come. Everyone knows anyway."

Outside their quarters Dick Cutler, a tall thin man, was standing beside jeep #7. He had his camera on his shoulder. When he saw Jim coming out of the building, he ran and shook his hand," Dick Cutler. I'm with Novak."

Lucky Seven

Jim pulled his hand free, "I didn't say both of you could come along."

"I just take the pictures. I'm sort of Novak's right arm. Part of him, you know, like Grabowsky here is to you."

Jim jumped in the Jeep. The others loaded in behind him. Jim turned around, "Okay, but this is no circus. These are innocent people that need help."

"That's the only reason we want to tag along," Novak said climbing in.

Chuck started the Jeep. Twenties minutes later they drove into the village and found it deserted.

Novak noticed, "Where is everyone?"

"Probably at the temple," Chuck said. He drove on through the village and out into the jungle following the dirt trail towards the temple. When they reached the temple, it was overflowing with people. Many of them were in groups outside.

Chuck pulled up. They were greeted by Taylor who took them inside.

"People come from far away to see Jesus heal people," Taylor said. He proudly led Jim inside and up to the altar.

Cutler had his camera rolling and moved around the temple.

Novak and Chuck remain by the entrance whispering.

"Did you know you have VC here?" Novak asked.

"How can you tell?"

"That's the scuttlebutt at the base. How many bullet wounds has he healed?"

"Actually, quite a number, but we thought they were regular village people caught in a firefight somewhere."

Novak looked around, "I'd say you have at least twenty or more VC here."

"Taylor said people have been coming in from the other villages, but VC?"

"They have plenty of wounded too," Novak said. "You don't want to be here when the brass figures it out. You know aiding and abetting the enemy is not good."

"They haven't said he couldn't heal them."

Novak watched as the people were being healed, "That's because they didn't believe he could, but he has the gift all right. Look at him! It has to be protected and used in the right way, or it will destroy him."

"That's where you come in?"

"No, that's where you come in. I'm only going to report what I see."

Suddenly a jet plane flew low over the building. The loud noise caused it to shake.

Novak looked around nervously, "I think that's a hint we should be moving along."

Chuck looked at his watch, "Yes, it's time we headed back." He went up and whispered to Jim, "Let's go!"

Jim glanced up and nodded. He healed one more person and then eased himself up. He found his legs a bit wobbly.

Christopher Charles

Chuck moved people aside to allow Jim to move through the crowd coming out. Jim had his arm around Taylor. When they reached the Jeep, Jim gave Taylor a big hug. Chuck climbed in the other side and started the motor. Cutler loaded his camera into the Jeep and climbed in beside Novak.

Jim with Taylor clinging said, "I'll come back. You'll see. It's only two months."

Taylor had tears in his eyes, "You go away like Taylor dad, and never come back. You forget Taylor."

Jim hugged Taylor again, "I can't ever forget you. You were my first gift."

"Taylor yours forever?"

"Yes, Taylor is mine forever. We will go home together when I leave for good."

Taylor smiled, "You will take Taylor then?"

"Yes."

"Then Taylor let you go for short time now."

Taylor freed Jim and allowed him to climb into the jeep.

Lucky Seven

Jim shouted, "I'll be back!" As the Jeep drove away.

9 Home

When Jim and Chuck boarded their flight to come home, they found Novak and Cutler on the same military flight. Once they reached the United States, they switched to a commercial flight and ended up at the Burbank Airport.

Jim and Chuck walked off the plane in full uniform carrying their duffle bags on their shoulders. Behind them came Novak and Cutler carrying their suitcases.

Jim stopped by a shop selling flowers and picked up a handful of lilies. He turned to Chuck and smiled, "For Crystal."

Cutler bought several newspapers and stuffed them under his arm. The four men came out of the terminal door. A taxi pulled up. The driver threw their luggage into the trunk as they climbed into the taxi.

The driver slipped into his seat, turned, and asked, "Where to?"

"The Presbyterian Church on Bernard," Jim said. Holding his flowers. He leaned back and took a deep breath.

Cutler scanned the papers, "Novak's got you in four out of five papers. You can expect your church to be packed."

"What?" Chuck asked taking the papers. He looked through them quickly, "Novak has you plastered all over the front page."

Jim took the papers from Chuck, looked at them, turned to Novak, "You did this?"

"It sells papers. I think your girlfriend knows you're coming."

"Yes, but not like this. I think we need to part company, Novak."

"Suit yourself, but I've only told them what you are. So, I made you a little popular."

"I rather not be popular."

Christopher Charles

"You're not going to be able to hide this gift. You have to deal with it. Better a friend tells the story."

"Friend? A friend wouldn't do this." Jim tossed the papers.

Novak shrugged his shoulders.

At the Presbyterian Church a large crowd had gather outside, most of them were the media. The church ushers were keeping them outside. They did not notice the taxi pulling up. Chuck, stepped out of the taxi, paid the driver, who deposited their duffle bags on the sidewalk. Jim picked up his bag, started for the church, and then stopped to wait for Chuck.

Novak remained in the taxi, but he stuck his head out the window, "If you change your mind, you can reach me through my paper."

Jim ignored him and started for the building. He heard Crystal singing inside the church. He turned and shouted to Chuck, "Come on, that's her."

Chuck looked at Novak departing. Turning, he ran to catch up with Jim, "You're right, her voice is beautiful."

Lucky Seven

As they approached the church entrance, a reporter discovered them, "There he is!" He ran up to Jim, "Are you going to heal people today? Is that why you are here?"

"Later. Later. Let us through please", Chuck yelled pushing the reporter away.

"Are you here to meet Crystal Hundly?" Another reporter asked.

Jim and Chuck reached the door. Chuck held back the reporters, but a cameraman ducked in around him.

Jim entered the church. The media followed him with their light bulbs flashing. People turned towards him. He dropped his duffle bag at the door, but he kept the lilies and searched for a place to sit.

Crystal, her tears flowing, stopped singing. She motioned for Jim to come to the podium.

Gottschalk, sitting on the platform, immediately stood and moved next to Crystal. He took her wrist and started to whisper in her ear. Crystal broke free and ran from the platform to Jim.

Christopher Charles

Jim and Crystal embraced in the aisle with the reporter's cameras clicking and the people cheering.

Jim released Crystal and handed her the lilies, "Love you, I brought you these."

"Thank you. Thank you for coming home." Crystal took the flowers, pulled Jim close and kissed him on the lips.

The congregation clapped and cheered.

The kiss finished, Crystal took Jim by the hand and led him towards the platform, "Come on!"

Gottschalk glared at Jim through a fixed smile, stepped to the podium, "Now, who you all have been waiting for, Reverend James Baughman. I know there is some of you who have come praying Jesus will touch you. We have heard God has given Jim the gift. Maybe we can impose upon him today."

Gottschalk pushed Jim to the podium and tried to gently move Crystal back.

Crystal refused to let go of Jim, "I'm staying with him."

Lucky Seven

Gottschalk whispered to Crystal, "It could be dangerous."

Crystal glared back at Gottschalk and stayed with Jim.

Jim turned to Crystal, "You really want me to do this now. This is your service."

"It ceased being my service when I opened my door this morning to a hallway full of reporters." She paused a second, "It's safe, isn't it?"

Jim smiled, "No one has died yet." He glanced at the size of the audience, and continued, "I've never done it in front of a church crowd before."

Members of the audience began to make their way toward the front of the church.

Crystal looked up at Jim, "You don't have to do it now. I can tell them you're tired from your trip."

"No, Gottschalk is hoping I'll call it off."

"Or fail! Maybe you should wait until you feel better."

Christopher Charles

"It will work now as well as later. I've been tired before."

Jim turned, faced the crowd, and stepped to the podium. Crystal held his left hand. Jim raised his right hand, "Let's pray! Jesus. Jesus. Fill my hands with your healing power. Let me be your instrument. Let your Holy Spirit heal these people."

An arthritic old lady moved out into the aisle and steadied herself with her walker. She looked up at Jim, lifted one arm, and cried, "I need a healing Reverend. My old bones have been hurting me something awful."

The Arthritic Old Lady's weak left hand caused her to lose her walker. She dropped to the floor.

Jim ran from the platform with Crystal in tow and knelt beside the Arthritic Old Lady.

The old lady looked up, "Help me, please!"

Jim held Crystal's hand, laid his right hand on the Arthritic Old Lady's back, "It will be Jesus who heals you."

Lucky Seven

Jim closed his eyes and prayed: "Jesus! Jesus! Heal this woman! Take away her pain."

The Arthritic Old Lady screamed. Crystal fainted and dropped to the floor. Jim started to reach for the Arthritic Old Lady.

She shoved him away shouting, "Don't touch me! Don't touch me!"

Arthritic Old Lady stood and ran out of the church. Chuck followed her. Three more would-be sick people quickly stood and left.

Jim knelt beside Crystal and took her hand. The congregation hushed into silence.

Gottschalk ran from the platform, yelling; "Don't touch her! Don't touch her!"

Jim gently lifted Crystal into his arms. Crystal opened her eyes and smiled as Gottschalk arrived.

Standing over them, Gottschalk yelled, "What did you do to her?"

Jim looked up, "I think she felt the healing power of the Holy Spirit."

Christopher Charles

Slowly Crystal regained her legs and smiled. Her legs suddenly gave out, she reached for Jim, "I think I have had enough for one day."

Gottschalk quickly walked to the podium. He raised his hands to the murmuring crowd, "I think we have over-taxed the two of them. This is the first time Crystal has seen him in nine months. I think it is best we allow them to rest a few days. Crystal will be back next Sunday. Maybe we can persuade Reverend Baughman to be with us too."

Gottschalk clapped. The crowd quickly took it up and continued to clap.

An usher with a mike in his ear motioned for Jim to follow him. Carrying Crystal, Jim followed the usher to Gottschalk's office. He placed her on the couch.

Crystal appeared weak as she sat with her flowers in her lap. Jim sat beside her and held her close.

Gottschalk entered, turned to the Usher, "No one is to enter here for the next few minutes."

Jim interrupted him, saying, "A friend of mine will be looking for me. He's in army fatigues."

Lucky Seven

"Okay, let him in, but no one else," Gottschalk said.

The Usher nodded and closed the door.

Gottschalk turned to Crystal. He dropped to one knee in front of her and took her hand. He gave Jim a hard stare, and asked, "What did you do to her?

"I don't know. It never happened before."

"I'm okay, honest," Crystal said. "I'll be fine in a minute."

"You sure?" Gottschalk asked.

"Yes. Yes. It was the weirdest feeling. I felt this energy go through me. I just wasn't prepared for it."

Crystal pulled her hand back from Gottschalk, and sat up, "I'll be all right."

Gottschalk stood, moved back, "I still think you should see a doctor."

"I said, I'm fine." She snuggled in closer to Jim, looked up at him, "You said we could get married when you came back."

Christopher Charles

"Yes, I did!" Jim looked up at Gottschalk, "Can you arrange it?"

"Yes, but Mrs. Hundly is not going to like it." He looked at Crystal, "You sure about this Crystal?"

"Yes, yes, I want to get married this week before something happens to change things."

"Your mother will want a big wedding. You should at least give her that."

"I'm the one getting married." She looked at Jim, "Is tomorrow okay?"

"Anytime is okay with me."

"You will have to wait until Thursday to make it legal," Gottschalk said, "But I can arrange it."

"Then Thursday, mother will just have to accept it."

There was a knock at the door. Gottschalk opened it.

The Usher leaned inside, "There's a Lieutenant Grabowsky here."

Rev. Gottschalk turned Jim's direction.

Lucky Seven

Jim nodded.

Gottschalk nodded to the Usher, and the door opened.

Crystal stood with Jim's help.

Chuck entered, he noticed Crystal and introduced himself, "Hi, I'm Chuck Grabowsky. Jim and I fly together."

Crystal gave Chuck her right hand, and started to say, "I'm..."

Chuck interrupted, "Crystal, yes! Jim didn't say how beautiful you are."

"I did too!"

"No, only how beautiful your voice is, but it's all of you. You radiate beauty. Say you don't love this man, and I will try my hand."

"Sorry, it's just Jim," Crystal said, "We are getting married Thursday."

"Congratulations Jim me boy," Chuck said. "Maybe now he will stop talking about you all the time." He winked at Jim.

"He does?"

Christopher Charles

Jim, embarrassed, became serious, "What did you find out?"

"You want to know right here?"

"Let's keep it out in the open."

"She was a plant. A set up here by your friend." He nodded towards Gottschalk.

"Who was a plant?" Crystal asked.

"The screaming Old Arthritic Lady who ran from the church. I think you gave her the fear of God because she couldn't wait to confess."

Crystal looked at Gottschalk, "Say you didn't."

"I couldn't take the chance."

"How many plants did you place?" Jim asked.

"They all left after the first one screamed."

"You didn't have to do that," Jim said, "It's real."

"That's yet to be seen, isn't it?"

There was a knock at the door. Gottschalk opened the door slightly and the Usher whispered in his ear. Gottschalk nodded, closed the door, and turned back, "They won't leave."

"Who?" Jim asked.

"Those that wanted to be healed," Gottschalk said. "There's about thirty of them. They won't leave until you come back."

"Then let's do it," Jim said.

"You sure you're up to it?" Crystal asked.

"Yes, I can do it. It'll be easier now that the crowd is gone."

The news people are still here," Gottschalk said. "They're probably the ones who are making the biggest fuss."

Jim shrugged his shoulders, moved toward the door, "They will always be here."

When they entered the sanctuary, people were lined up in the aisle. Some of them laid on the floor. Others occupied the pews beside the aisle.

Jim worked his way through them until he came to a cripple woman. He prayed for her. She passed out in his arms. Slowly the Cripple

Christopher Charles

Woman recovered, smiled, and stood slowly with Jim's help. Seeing herself standing, she broke out in tears. She gave Jim a big hug.

Jim helped the cured Cripple Woman to a pew and moved on to the next person.

The reporters descended on the Cripple Woman taking pictures and asking questions.

Gottschalk sent his ushers in to move them back.

Chuck was standing beside Crystal watching Jim work, "I should be taking him out of here today before the media has a field day with him."

"Where would you take him?" Crystal asked.

"I haven't seen my folks yet. Maybe we can hide out there until Thursday."

"Then I want to come too," Crystal said.

"Sure, if it's okay with your boss."

"Reverend Gottschalk? It will be okay."

"Then you're more than welcome."

Crystal smiled, "Thank you."

Lucky Seven

Jim touched a deformed man. He screamed and ran from the hall.

Crystal gave Gottschalk a hard stare.

He shrugged his shoulders.

She looked at Chuck, "Another faker."

"Probably."

"How long can he do that?"

"You mean heal people?"

"Yes."

"Each time he does it, it takes something out of him. After about twenty people, I try to make him stop."

"If they don't give him any rest, what could happen?"

"I've seen him lose conscious. He'll be very close to that before he finishes here unless we can pull him away before then."

Crystal looked up at Chuck, "He's lucky to have a friend like you." She gave Chuck a hug.

Christopher Charles

Later:

Jim worked his way through thirty people, healing them. He was exhausted. Chuck tried several times to get Jim to stop, but he wanted to do one more.

Finally, Chuck went to Gottschalk, "We've got to get him out of here. He can't take anymore."

"Yes, I'll take care of it," Gottschalk said, and nodded to his usher to bring the limousine to the front of the church.

Chuck went to Jim kneeling in front of the last person healed, "That's enough Jim me boy. It's time to go. There is another day. They have Gottschalk limo out front." He lifted Jim to his feet.

"Is there anymore," Jim asked.

"It doesn't matter, this is all you can handle," Chuck said, and led Jim towards the door. The limousine was waiting with Crystal inside. Chuck eased Jim in, and climbed in himself.

Jim, in the back seat, went into a comatose state. His head moved to Crystal's shoulder.

Lucky Seven

Chuck, sitting in the jump seat, turned to the driver, "Take us to Chino. Take the ten to Central Ave and go south."

The driver nodded. Chuck closed the driver's window.

Crystal was close to tears, "Look at him Chuck. He's barely breathing."

"He'll be like that until he's slept ten hours," Chuck said.

"We should have pulled him away earlier."

"I think the news people were pushing him," Chuck said. "They probably emptied the local hospital."

"You sure we've lost the news people?"

"That was part of the deal. We allowed them to take their pictures and they gave us our freedom this week."

Crystal nudged Jim, he didn't move. She cuddled him, "I don't think he can take anymore. You sure your folks will want us?"

Christopher Charles

"I've already talked to them. It's all set. It was nice of Reverend Gottschalk to give us his driver for the week."

"I told him we needed it for the wedding," Crystal said. "I agreed to have Jim back next Sunday. At least we will have each other for a few days."

Forty-Five minutes later the limousine was in Chino driving down a narrow dairy road.

Deep drainage ditches ran on each side of the narrow blacktop road. Small bridges over the ditches connected the long driveways. Dairy cows filled the landscape. The limousine turned off the main road and moved up a long driveway leading to a ranch style house. It passed cars and trucks parked on the side of the road.

Jim was asleep on Crystal's shoulder.

Crystal looked out the window, "I thought you made a deal with the press."

"This isn't the press. These are the neighbors."

"I thought we would have some privacy."

Lucky Seven

"They're just curious is all. I'll have dad send them on their way."

The limousine pulled up in front of Grabowsky's house. People filled the yard in front of the porch. The local press took pictures as the limousine pulled up.

Neil Grabowsky, Chuck's father, a big man, stepped to the limousine and opened the door. He took a hug from his son climbing out, "Nice to have you home, son. I like your style."

Mary Grabowsky, Chuck's mother, heavyset and middle age, pushed her husband to one side, "Let me have my son." She hugged him until her tears flowed. She wiped them, stepped back, "Now, who did you bring home?"

Chuck helped Crystal emerged from the limousine, "This is Crystal Hundly, mother. Crystal this is Mary, my mother, and Neil, my father."

Neil stepped forward and gave Crystal a big hug.

Mary pushed him away, "You leave her be. Maybe she's not Chuck's girl."

Christopher Charles

"Just being sociable to the prettiest girl next to you I've ever seen."

"She belongs to Jim," Chuck said. "They're getting married Thursday." He nodded towards the car.

Crystal gave a faint smile, turned, and helped Jim emerge from the car. Jim appeared disoriented.

The crowd behind them stirred and moved in closer.

Chuck quickly took Jim's other arm and helped him step out of the car. Jim stood a moment adjusting himself.

Neil shook Jim's limp hand, "Sure glad to meet you, sir. These people have been waiting most of the morning for you."

Jim looked up slightly, "Nice to meet you."

Chuck turned to his dad, "We were hoping to stay here a few days for some rest."

"No problem son. We'll be glad to have them here a spell, right mother."

Lucky Seven

"Yes, you know your friends are always welcome."

Crystal bowed slightly, "Thank you." She turned to Jim, "Come along dear. You can rest inside." She led Jim towards the house. She had to push her way through the crowd until the crowd became too dense. She finally stopped, looked back at Chuck, "We've got to get him inside. He's very tired."

"We were hoping he would heal some of the folks first," Neil said. "Your Aunt Martha has come all this way. You know her arthritis has been hurting her something awful."

"He's really exhausted dad, maybe tomorrow."

Jim found some strength, stood up more, "I'll try some. I still feel the energy inside of me."

The people pressed in closer. Chuck pushed them back, yelling, "Only one at a time! One at a time!"

The people moved into a line behind Aunt Martha, a woman in her late sixties. Mary brought a chair from the house. Jim slowly sat and motioned for Aunt Martha to come closer.

Christopher Charles

Aunt Martha timidly approached Jim, "You're not going to hurt me, are you?"

"No, only heal you."

Jim took Aunt Martha's hand as she knelt in front of him. He rubbed his hand down and across her back, "Heal! Heal her Jesus."

Aunt Martha stared at Jim a moment, smiled, and then stood. She turned to the crowd yelling, "I'm healed! I'm healed!"

Jim smiled, and motioned for the next one. He continued to see three more until Chuck came in to his rescue, "That's all for today folks, Jim needs his rest. He lifted Jim from the chair and took him into the house.

Mary hurried in front of him leading Chuck and Jim to the empty bedroom. Jim collapsed on the bed. They placed a blanket over him and allowed him to finally rest.

The next day Crystal was in the kitchen talking to her mother on the kitchen phone.

Phone:

"Yes mother, This Thursday 3:30 P.M. at the church."

Pause:

"Please don't faint mother."

Pause:

"Yes, I know it is sudden. It is either that or a quick wedding."

Pause:

"Yes, Reverend Gottschalk will do the ceremony."

Pause:

"We're getting the license today. I have to run. I will talk to you later, mother."

Crystal turned as Jim entered the kitchen.

He looked better after sleeping ten hours and taking a shower. "What did she say?"

"You don't want to know. She doesn't like you right now, but that will change after we're married."

"And the wedding?"

Christopher Charles

"She will have everyone there. She has been planning this for years. She even has my dress hanging in the closet."

Jim smiled, took her into his arms, gave her a hug, "At least I am not sporting a beard. That should make her happy."

Crystal ran her hand along his face, "It makes me happy." Then she pushed herself away and pulled him towards the door. "Come on," She yelled. "Chuck is already outside. We need to pick up our wedding license."

"Reverend Gottschalk?"

"We're picking him up on the way."

They climbed into the limousine. Chuck was already inside. Forty minutes later they picked up Gottschalk at the church. He sat in the jump seat beside Chuck across from Crystal and Jim holding hands.

Gottschalk pulled an envelope from his coat pocket, handed it to Crystal, "This makes you legally married except for the ceremony."

Lucky Seven

"Thank you for making things easy," Crystal said. She leaned forward and kissed Gottschalk on the cheek.

Gottschalk, embarrassed, gently pushed her back, turned to Jim, "We haven't really seen how effective your gift is. Maybe we should give it a real test."

"Like what?" Jim asked.

"Maybe we could go to the hospital and heal those in intensive care."

"No, no, we've tried that," Chuck said.

"That was the army," Jim said. "It will be different here."

Gottschalk turned to the driver, "Take us to the Community Hospital."

When they arrived at the hospital, the three of them entered, and walked to the intensive ward unit. They found the nurse's station. It occupied the center of a circular room with ten patients on the life support system.

The station nurse was scanning the ten monitors coming from the patients. She would

Christopher Charles

read the monitors, and then record the numbers in the patient's chart.

When Gottschalk and company entered, she looked up, "What can I do for you?"

Gottschalk leaned on the counter, "I am Reverend Gottschalk from the Presbyterian Church. We would like to pray for the patients." He handed the Station Nurse his business card.

She looked at it, nodded, "Go ahead. If anyone needs praying for these people certainly do. Four of them will not make the day."

"Thank you," Gottschalk said, smiled and nudged Jim towards the first patient, an unconscious Balding Man in his sixties.

The Station Nurse went back to her paperwork and ignored them.

Jim walked to the man. He stood over him, closed his eyes and prayed a moment. Then he took the Balding Man's arm full of tubes sticking out and looked at Crystal who nodded for him to go ahead.

"Let Jesus heal them," She whispered.

Lucky Seven

Jim turned to the unconscious Balding Man and quietly prayed, "Heal him Jesus. Heal him."

Nothing happened. Jim prayed again with more emphasis, "Heal him Jesus! Heal him!"

Jim waited a few more seconds, but nothing happened. The Balding Man remained unconscious. Jim closed his eyes tighter, then shouting quietly, he said, "Heal him Jesus! Heal him!"

The Balding Man moved and opened his eyes. He started to raise his head.

Jim smiled, and eased the man back to his pillow, "Sh...Sh... Don't say anything. You've just been healed."

The Balding Man nodded.

Jim patted the man on the leg and moved to the next unconscious patient.

Crystal smiled and looked at Gottschalk.

Gottschalk whispered, "He has nine more."

At the nurse's station Chuck glanced at the monitors changing to "normal" as Jim prayed for

Christopher Charles

the patients. The Station Nurse recorded the monitor of the patient Jim had not seen yet.

Chuck noticed, and moved closer to the Station Nurse, "This must be a depressing job."

"Yes, at times it is very hard," the nurse said, "So many die here."

"How would you feel if everyone suddenly left today alive and well."

"That would be something of a miracle."

"Say it happened?" Chuck asked.

The station nurse shook her head, "That's not possible." She turned back to her monitors and noticed the changes. She looked back at her previous notes and then at the monitors again. She struck the Balding Man's monitor with her pen, but it did not change. She looked up to see the Balding Man sitting and smiling at her.

The Balding Man lifted his arm indicating he wanted the tubes taken out.

The Station Nurse surveyed the room. The other patients wanted their tubes out. She saw Jim praying for the last unconscious patient, "What's he doing to them?"

Lucky Seven

"Healing them," Chuck said.

The Station Nurse picked up her phone, yelling, "Blue cart stat! Security stat!" Then she replaced the phone, turned to Chuck screaming, "Stop him! Stop him!"

Chuck went to Jim as the last patient regained consciousness, "I think it's time we leave, Jim-me-boy. She has called security."

Jim looked up. He appeared weak and haggard. He nodded and allowed Chuck to lead him from the room. Crystal followed with a concern look on her face. Gottschalk ducked his head when he passed the nurse's station.

The Station Nurse yelled after them, "Don't you dare leave here! What did you do to them?"

Two doctors and four nurses came running in with the blue cart. They looked at the patients sitting up and then back at the Station Nurse.

She pointed to the departing three disappearing down the hallway, "Them!"

The doctors looked at her with a puzzled look as two security officers came rushing in.

Christopher Charles

Down in the parking lot the limousine pulled away. A lone security officer came out the door and took down the license number. Forty minutes later the limousine pulled into the Grabowsky long driveway.

People, waiting in cars and trucks, occupied all the available parking space. The limousine moved through them and pulled up in front of the house. People left their cars and started toward the house.

The limousine dropped off Jim, Crystal, and Chuck, and worked its way back out the drive with Gottschalk inside.

Mary came out of the house, "How did it go?"

"He healed them," Crystal shouted. "He healed them all! You should have seen Reverend Gottschalk's face."

Chuck, walking towards the house said, "I think it was a bad idea. That nurse didn't seem all that pleased about it."

"They were healed," Jim said. "That's all that's important. I'm sure the patients appreciated it."

Chuck turned to Jim, "How you feeling?"

"They about drained everything out of me, but I'm okay now."

"These people have been waiting all morning for you," Mary said.

Jim looked at Crystal.

"It's okay if you're up to it."

Jim nodded.

Two days later

Chuck was on the phone in the Grabowsky's kitchen. He was facing the wall, "Thanks Ken, I appreciate it."

Crystal entered as Chuck hung up. He turned around and asked, "How's he doing?"

"He hasn't eaten anything in two days. He can barely raise his head. He can't do this anymore. He can't!" Crystal sobbed as Chuck took her into his arms.

Neil entered from the outside shaking his head, "You've got to get him out of here. They just keep coming, and they won't leave. How can a man get his chores done when his barn's full of people?"

Christopher Charles

Mary entered, took Crystal from Chuck, "There dear, it's just a little hard right now." She glared at her husband, "He's doing God's work. He can stay as long as he wants to."

"A man can't say who lives in his house anymore," Neil said stomping from the kitchen.

"It's okay," Chuck said, "I've called Ken over at the sheriff's office. He's coming over to move everyone out."

Neil from the outside yelled over his shoulder, "It can't be too soon for me. I've always liked that kid."

10 Thursday: The Wedding Day

The limousine was traveling to the Presbyterian Church in Pasadena with Crystal in her wedding dress sitting next to Jim in his tux.

Chuck, wearing a tux, sat across from them, and said, "This is the big day."

"Yes," Crystal said. She turned to Jim, "You okay?"

"Yes, thanks to Chuck's friend, Ken. All I needed was a little rest."

The limousine phone rang.

Chuck picked it up. He turned to Crystal, handed her the phone, "It's Reverend Gottschalk, for you."

Crystal took the phone, spoke into it, "Yes."

Gottschalk on the other end of the line was talking into a payphone, "You can't go to the church. The newspapers have been playing up Jim's miracle work at the hospital. The church is overflowing with people. It looks dangerous. I have the police there, but they're saying you can't go there."

"Mother?" Crystal asked.

"You better leave her be," Gottschalk said. "She is very upset right now. If you want to be married today, it will have to be done in the limousine. No place is safe now."

Crystal turned to Jim with tears in her eyes. "He says we have to be married in the Limousine."

"It's okay by me. I didn't want a big wedding anyway."

Crystal turned back to the phone, "Okay."

"I'm at the hospital, pick me up here."

Crystal handed the phone back to Chuck, "Reverend Gottschalk wants us to pick him up at the hospital."

Lucky Seven

Chuck hung up phone, turned to driver, "Hospital."

A few minutes later the limousine pulled into the hospital parking lot. They see Gottschalk waiting for them. They pulled into a parking space, and Gottschalk stepped into the limousine.

They remained in the parking lot as Gothschalk took Jim and Crystal through their marriage vows. When he was finished, he smiled, "And now you may kiss the bride."

Jim and Crystal kissed.

She turned back beaming.

Chuck leaned over, "Now it's my turn." He kissed Crystal on the cheek.

Crystal turned to Gottschalk and gave him a big hug, "Thank you for everything."

Gottschalk pushed her back and became very solemn, "You may not be thanking me after I tell you what has happened."

He turned to the driver, "Take us to the Presbyterian Church." Then he pulled out a newspaper and handed it to Chuck. He looked at Jim, "Two of your patients died that you healed at the hospital after they went home. Two others almost died, but they managed to reach the hospital in time."

Jim looked at Gottschalk, "You sure?"

Chuck was turning the pages of the newspaper, "It's all here in the paper."

Jim dropped back against the seat.

"That's one of the reasons why I was at the hospital," Gottschalk said. "It checks. They showed me the dead bodies. It is also the main reason you could not be married at the church."

Pause:

"They don't want you coming near it. They have a restraining order." Gottschalk reached into his coat pocket, withdrew a legal letter, handed it to Chuck, "I am being sued along with the church and hospital."

"What about Jim?" Crystal asked.

"He's still army," Gottschalk said. "They probably will be liable."

Jim whispered out loud, "They were healed when we left."

"It was the hospital that allowed them to go home," Chuck said.

"Yes, that was my argument, but why did it happen, Jim?"

"I don't know. Maybe they were supposed to die. I just delayed it some."

"Has it ever happened before?" Gottschalk asked.

"I don't know," Jim looked at Chuck.

"We never did any follow up," Chuck said. "We have always assumed they were healed."

"I need some answers here. I'm facing an angry church board in a moment. Crystal's and my future hangs on what I say."

"What do you want me to do?" Jim asked.

Chuck shoved the newspaper towards Jim. "It says here your gift may not be of God. They're saying it isn't Biblical."

"I feel his Holy Spirit and heal people," Jim said.

Christopher Charles

Jesus healed by faith," Gottschalk said. "They believed he was God. That faith healed them. You seem to heal people who don't even know who Jesus is."

"We've have always tried to tell the people who was healing them," Jim said.

"Really, I didn't hear you tell any of those you healed in the hospital who did the healing."

"They were unconscious to start with," Jim said, "And there wasn't time afterward. But I have always healed in Jesus' name."

"Why are you so tired afterward?" Gottschalk asked. "Jesus was never tired."

"That's just what it does to me. I feel this enormous energy fill my body. When I touch someone, it drains out and heals them. It weakens me each time the energy flows out."

"There's been no record in the Bible of someone becoming weak after the Holy Spirit touches them," Gottschalk said.

"I don't think there is any record of how the disciples felt after they healed someone, and well Jesus was God wasn't he?" Crystal said.

Lucky Seven

"Maybe you're right, Reverend Gottschalk," Jim said. "Jesus healed people who sought healing. I've healed people who had nothing to say about it."

"Does that mean you've done something wrong in God's eyes?" Chuck asked.

"I don't know. I've healed a lot of people without their consent."

The limousine pulled up in front of the police barricades in front of the Presbyterian Church. The police made an opening and the limousine passed through and parked. Gottschalk opened his door, "I'll see what I can do about saving our jobs. A little prayer might help."

Crystal gave him a quick hug, "Sorry, I wish I could help."

"Just don't do anymore healing," Gottschalk said stepping out of the car.

Forty minutes later

The limousine was approaching the long driveway leading up to the Grabowsly's house in Chino. It moved slowly between the parked trucks and cars on the road.

Christopher Charles

Crystal turned to Jim, "These people believe in you."

Just then, a ripe tomato struck the windshield and splattered across it.

"Better move it," Chuck said. "I see the sheriff's car up ahead."

More tomatoes struck the car covering most of the windows as the limousine pulled into the long drive. The Sheriff's barricade was just ahead of them. The limousine quickly passed through and pulled up beside a military car in front of the house. Chuck leaped from the limousine and ran for the porch door. Jim helped Crystal out.

A teenage boy ran past the Sheriff's barricade and threw a tomato. It bounced off the car and splattered Crystal's white wedding dress.

Mary started to open the door kitchen door when the three of them burst through. She gave Crystal a hug, "You poor dear. We've been watching the news."

Crystal cried, "Everything has been so awful. They've ruined my dress."

Lucky Seven

Mary gently pushed Crystal back to look at her dress, "It will come out. Now don't you worry none. We have the Sheriff and the army's here. No one can hurt you now."

Chuck looked around, "What's the army doing here?"

Two army officers entered the room. The First Officer pulled several sheets of paper from his coat pocket, and asked, "Lieutenant Grabowsky and Baughman?"

Jim and Chuck nodded.

"We have orders to take you with us," The First Officer said.

Crystal ran into Jim's arms, turned to the officers, "Where are you taking him?"

The First Officer looked at the papers, then at Crystal, "Vietnam, ma'am."

Crystal buried her head into Jim's shoulder and cried.

Outside an old pickup truck was approaching fast. It barreled into the Sheriff's barriers and sent them high into the air. It came to a skidding stop. The Truck Driver leaped to the ground. He reached inside the truck and brought out a limp Little Girl. He glanced back at the approaching sheriffs and ran towards the house.

Chuck opened the door. The Truck Driver charged in, he saw Jim, and pushed pass Chuck. He dropped to his knees and lifted the limp Little Girl up to Jim, and pleaded, "Bring her back to life. She's all I have. Please bring her back to life."

Crystal moved back.

Jim dropped beside the Truck Driver, "How long ago did she die?"

"A few minutes ago, at the hospital," he said. "She had leukemia. You can save her. Please!"

"Jesus can," Jim said.

"I wouldn't advise doing that, sir," The First Officer said.

Jim gave the First Officer a hard stare and turned to the Little Girl. He took her from the Truck Driver, held her close, and prayed, "Heal her Jesus like you did Taylor. Heal her for this man's faith."

Lucky Seven

Jim falls forward. He was unable to move. Then slowly he handed the Little Girl back to the Truck Driver.

The Little Girl opened her eyes, smiled, and said, "Papa. Papa."

The Truck Driver squeezed his Little Girl. Tears roll down his cheeks, "Thank you. Thank you."

Jim remained on his knees. He held himself as he began to shake.

Crystal dropped down beside him, "It's okay. It's okay."

"We have to be going sir," the First Officer said.

Jim nodded, and forced himself to stand with Crystal's help. He suddenly looked very tired and haggard.

Mary gave him some tea.

He took a few sips, "Thanks, I feel better."

Christopher Charles

Ten minutes later

Jim and Chuck changed into their military uniform, picked up their duffle bags and placed them in the military car. Jim looked up at the officer, "Is it okay if Crystal comes along with us."

The First Officer thought a second, then shaking his head, "We're taking you to a military transport. You better say good-byes here."

Crystal hugged Jim, kissed him passionately, "I love you, please come back."

"I will when things settle down."

She pulled back, looked him in the eyes, "No matter what happens, you come back to me."

She moved back into Jim's arms that collapsed over her.

Jim pulled her closer, "I love you. I love you."

"Please come back," Crystal said in his ear. "We can deal with this together. I love you so very much."

The First Military Officer was becoming impatient, "We have to make that transport."

Lucky Seven

Chuck pulled Jim away saying, "We've got to go, Jim."

Jim nodded, gently pushed Crystal away and climbed into the military car.

The military car moved slowly through the crowd as it gave way in silence allowing the car to reach the road. Once free of the people the car picked up speed.

Christopher Charles

11 Viet Nam

The air force cargo plane landed and taxied up to a waiting crowd of men in fatigues. The stairs dropped. Jim and Chuck walked down to a waiting Jeep. Matthews sat behind the wheel and motioned for them to get in. The men in fatigues rushed up wanting to touch Jim as the Jeep started to move away. Corporal Digs, a short wiry man, ran up beside them, yelled, "Thanks for healing me. Thanks for making them believe."

Jim smiled and nodded to Digs as the Jeep accelerated forward and disappeared between the buildings. They arrived at Captain Bollinger's office. They followed Matthew into the building.

Outside of Captain Bollinger's office Matthew stopped, turned and said, "Wait here!" He knocked on the door.

Lucky Seven

Inside, Bollinger was puffing on his cigar and reading a report when he heard the knock.

Matthew stuck his head in, "They're here, sir."

"Send them in."

Jim and Chuck entered the office. Bollinger pointed to the two chairs in front of the desk as he continued to read the report.

"Lieutenant Baughman and Grabowsky reporting sir," Jim said as they sat in the chairs.

Bollinger ignored them a moment. Then he dropped his paperwork, looked at them hard, "I thought we sent you two on leave for two months?"

"I guess it didn't work out so well," Chuck said.

"You think we're going to hold your hand?"

"No sir," Jim said. "We just want to do our job."

"Good, cause that's all I want you to do. No more of this healing business in the field, on the base, or in the helicopter. You got that?"

"Yes sir," Chuck said.

Bollinger turned to Jim, "And you?"

"Yes sir. No more healing for the army."

"Good, now get the hell out of here."

Jim and Chuck quickly stood and left the office.

Matthew was waiting for them outside, and nodded, "Follow me."

They climbed into the jeep outside and sped across the airbase. Matthew took them away from the old barracks.

Chuck noticed, "Hey, we're over there."

"You've been moved to private quarters."

"We had private quarters," Chuck said. "Nobody else was there."

"It's full now. We didn't expect you back for two months, remember?"

The Jeep pulled up beside a lone bungalow on the outer fringes of the airbase. Their number seven Jeep was in the parking space outside the building. The temporary structure contained two beds and two lockers.

Matthews entered the building with a clipboard in one hand, and a radio pack in the other. Jim and Chuck followed carrying their duffle bags.

Matthew turned, "This is your new quarters gentlemen, and here is your duty roster." He dropped the radio pack on the floor and handed Chuck a sheet of paper. He continued, "Remember, standby means on the base at all times."

"Yeah, we know," Chuck said.

"Good, you're on standby today. Between you and me, there won't be any action until this afternoon. He turned to Jim, "It will give you a chance to rest."

"Thanks." Jim said.

Matthews, nodded, turned, and left. Jim and Chuck hung their duffle bags in the lockers.

Chuck turned, "We're back. It feels good to have some control over your life again."

They heard the Matthew's jeep leave.

Christopher Charles

Jim falls back on the bed and breathed in deep. "I'm still tired. I could sleep for a week."

There was a knock on the window. Jim sat up as Taylor came through the door.

"Taylor!" Chuck shouted. "What are you doing here? You could be shot."

Taylor flashed a smile and ran into Jim's arms, "They never catch Taylor."

Taking the hug, Jim asked, "How did you know we were here?"

"Everyone know you come back for Taylor."

"I came back, but you have to leave now. Chuck is right! They will shoot you on sight."

Taylor stood, "I'm not afraid. You come to Jesus temple now. Everyone wait for you."

"No, we're on standby today. It will have to be tomorrow. I will come tomorrow."

"How did you find us?" Chuck asked.

"I see number seven Jeep."

"Well, you're out of here now," Chuck said.

Lucky Seven

Taylor gave Jim another big hug, backed towards the door, "Tomorrow, you promise Taylor."

"Yes, tomorrow."

Taylor turned and ran out. Jim falls back on the bed.

Later that afternoon

Jim and Chuck stood in front of the #7 Helicopter on pad #3. They watched the soldiers coming out of the far building and walking toward the four helicopters warming up on pad #2.

Meade stood in front of the helicopters and waited for the men to fall in. Some of the men were already in front of him.

On pad #3 Chuck turned to Jim, "Remember, no healing this time."

"I know the order."

Corporal Digs looked at Jim as he walked towards pad #2. Digs stopped, glanced at Meade, and then ran to Jim, "I heard you can't heal us later, but can you pray for me now."

Christopher Charles

Jim looked at Chuck, and then at the Dig's insistent face, "He didn't say I couldn't pray for them."

Digs dropped his pack and knelt.

Jim placed his hands on Digs' head, and prayed, "Jesus. Jesus. Protect this man from the enemy's bullets. Give him your shield and sword."

Digs falls backward slightly and staggered to his feet, "I felt it! I felt it! Thank you. Thank you." He stood, picked up his pack, and ran towards Sergeant Meade.

The other men, watching, stopped, dropped their packs, ran to Jim, and said in unison, "Pray for us! Pray for us!"

Jim nodded. They all reach in and took hold of his clothes or body as he prayed, "Jesus. Jesus. Protect these men from the enemy's bullets. Give them your shield and sword."

The men stood in shock. They looked at each other and felt their arms. Breaking out into a smile, one man gave Jim a hug. The others quickly followed slapping Jim wherever they could.

Lucky Seven

Then noticing Meade staring at them, the men quickly picked up their packs and ran toward their helicopters.

On Pad #2 the men in line waiting to board the helicopters looked at Meade with pleading eyes.

"Okay, go," Mead said, "Let's see how well his voodoo works."

The men dropped their packs in place and ran to Jim. The prayed-for men arrived smiling and full of confidence.

"Next time you do this on your time not the army's," Meade yelled. "Now board! We've got a war to fight."

The other men returned, picked up their packs, and followed the others aboard the helicopters. Meade gave Jim a hard look.

"I prayed for you too sergeant," Jim yelled over.

Meade waved him off and climbed aboard a helicopter. Immediately the four helicopters lifted off and disappeared.

Christopher Charles

On pad #3 Chuck turned to Jim, "It's time we were moving."

Jim nodded and climbed aboard the #7 helicopter.

In flight Jim and Chuck sat in their seats, staring out the windscreen, and talked in their helmet mikes.

"This is our second trip up and nothing," Jim said. "I don't think there's going to be any wounded tonight."

Chuck smiled, "This is better than healing them afterwards."

Then over the speaker came, "7 helicopter return to base, repeat, return to base."

"That's it. No wounded. A first I think," Jim said.

"Let's go home."

Evening the next day

Bollinger was looking over the battle report when Sergeant Meade entered the office.

"You've got to get rid of him," Meade shouted.

Lucky Seven

Bollinger lifted the report, "What's the problem? It says here he only prayed for them. You didn't have any causalities, did you?"

"No, that's the problem. I had no control. The men disobeyed my orders and ran straight into the enemy's fire. I was hoping one of them would take a bullet. I almost shot one of them myself. I want him out of here."

"It's being handled," Bollinger said. He pressed the intercom, "Matthews, where are Lieutenant Baughman and Grabowsky?"

"They're on call today sir. I would say they're in the village at some temple. That's where they usually go."

Bollinger leaned forward, spoke into the intercom, "You put them on standby and get them back here, now! We have an emergency."

"Yes sir," Matthew's said.

Bollinger dropped the intercom button, picked up the phone, "Colonel, Bollinger here, we have a problem, sir. I've got Baughman and Grabowsky at that temple."

Christopher Charles

Over phone Colonel Hardgrove said, "Get them out of there. Tell them the plane's coming in with no gear down. It's an emergency, damn you!"

"And if I can't get them out?"

"Then it is in God's hands, isn't it?"

"Yes sir," Bollinger said and hung up the phone. He pressed the intercom button, "Matthews, tell them a plane is coming in with landing gear failure. They have to come in now."

Over intercom Matthew said, "Yes sir, I have them on line."

Jim's was healing people inside the temple while Chuck stood by the Jeep talking into his radio mike.

Chuck dropped the radio in the Jeep and ran inside the temple. He saw Jim healing a young man with a bullet hole in his side, and Taylor standing to one side with the next wounded man. He ran up to them and waited for Jim to finish.

"Heal him Jesus. Heal him," Jim shouted.

The man stood and smiled.

Jim smiled back and turned to Chuck.

Lucky Seven

"We have to go. A plane is coming in with no gear down. It's an emergency. Bollinger said, now!"

Jim nodded, pulled Taylor close, "Taylor, I've got to go. Tell them I'll be back in an hour or so."

In Vietnamese Taylor said, "Jesus be back to heal more later. Base boss say emergency."

Jim, haggard and tired, nodded and walked slowly towards the door with Taylor following him. He gave Taylor a hug and falls into the running Jeep.

Chuck looked at Jim, "It's good we leave for a while. You need some time to recover."

"Taylor, keep everyone here until you come back."

Jim smiled slightly as he gave a slight wave of his hand. The Jeep whirled around and raced up the road.

The plane could be heard approaching.

Taylor stood in the road with tears streaming down his face, and softly said, "Bye Jesus."

Christopher Charles

The Jeep moved along the trail. Jim reached back and retrieved the radio. He pressed the on button.

The pilot of the approaching airplane was speaking on the radio speaker, "My gear won't drop. I'm coming in on my belly. I need to drop my load somewhere."

Over the radio, Bollinger asked, "Where are you?"

"I'm near that village by the base."

"Drop them before you get there. I don't want any civilian problems."

"Yes sir, dropping them now!"

Jim pushed the talk button, yelling, "No! No! Don't drop them! Civilians are here!"

The airplane flew over them as two loud explosions lift the Jeep high into the air. When the debris settled the Jeep was on its side against a tree. Chuck worked his way out of the Jeep.

Jim laid on the road. He forced himself to stand and looked around in a daze.

"You okay?" Chuck yelled.

Lucky Seven

Jim nodded slowly and started walking back towards the temple. His walk broke into a run when the flames become visible.

Chuck watched for a moment, then pushed the Jeep upright and inspected it.

At the temple flames consumed the structure.

Jim arrived breathing hard. When he approached the temple, an explosion inside the temple forced him to the ground. He slowly stood, yelling, "Taylor! Taylor!"

The flames moved into the jungle undergrowth forcing him further back. He stumbled backward over a lump in the high grass.

It was Taylor's burnt body.

Jim lifted the burnt body to his chest and prayed. "Jesus, Jesus, heal this body. Heal this body!"

Taylor opened his eyes and spoke through the pain, "Taylor not feel Jesus this time. Not feel Jesus."

"Nothing's coming through. Jesus! Jesus! Please heal him!"

Christopher Charles

Taylor whispered, "Not be healed second time. Hurt bad. Sorry Jesus, sorry."

Taylor died in Jim's arms as he slowly rocked back and forth. The fire was approaching his back.

Jim cried out, "Jesus, I don't feel you anymore. Why have you forsaken me?"

Pause:

Then in anguish, he cried, "Why did you let me heal them, if they were meant to die?" He dropped his head covering Taylor as another explosion went off in the temple sending debris into the grass around him.

The Jeep pulled up beside Jim. Chuck jumped out, yelling, "We've got to get out of here. The whole place is going up." He forced Jim to stand, but Jim refused to let go of Taylor's body. The grass was on fire around them.

Jim looked up, "I've got to bring him back to life. I've got to bring him back, Chuck."

"Okay, we take him with us." Chuck yelled helping Jim into the front seat. Coming around, he jumped in the driver's seat and drove the Jeep through the burning grass. The Jeep disappeared down the road as another loud explosion turned the grass into an inferno.

Chuck drove the Jeep towards the village while Jim held Taylor in his arms. Another explosion from the temple sent debris towards them, but it falls short.

"They must have had an ammunition dump below that temple," Chuck said.

Jim did not respond. His eyes remained fixed ahead.

The Jeep entered the deserted village, pulled up beside the Old Woman sitting on her steps.

She slowly stood, "Jesus bring Taylor inside."

Jim stumbled out of the Jeep carrying Taylor and followed the Old Woman inside. Chuck remained by the Jeep talking into his radio mike.

Jim entered the old-style Vietnamese house carrying Taylor. He gently laid Taylor on the bed and sat in the rocking chair facing the window.

The Old Woman moved to a small cabinet behind Jim. She lifted a covered vase of liquid and filled a glass. She pulled a small envelope from her pocket and dropped the contents into the glass. She stirred it and brought it to Jim.

"Here, drink this," she said, "It help Jesus find his soul."

Jim looked up, tried to smile, took the glass, and drank the total contents. Softly he said, "Thank you."

The Old Woman walked to the window and looked out, "Now Old Woman alone. Whole village die at temple. Soon I die then there will be no one."

Jim mumbled, "I couldn't save Taylor. There's nothing in me, it's all one big emptiness."

"Taylor already die. He lived for Jesus. Now no Jesus, he go away. When Jesus come back, maybe Taylor come back too." She retrieved the covered vase, stirred in another packet of powder, and filled Jim's glass.

Jim was about to drink it when Chuck entered the house.

Chuck knocked the glass from Jim's hands. The contents spilled on Jim's clothes. "Don't drink that! We're on standby tonight. We have to fly."

Lucky Seven

"It doesn't matter. Nothing matters now. I've lost it Chuck. Everything's gone. God has forsaken me."

Chuck whirled on the Old Woman, shouting, "What did you give him?"

"Something for his soul."

Jim rolled and falls forward in the chair.

Chuck caught him, "How much did you drink?"

Jim shook his head.

Chuck lifted Jim to his feet and started for the door. He stopped and turned to the Old Woman, "Well?"

The Old Woman ignored him and poured the contents of the vase into a glass. She lifted another packet from her pocket to show Chuck and emptied it into the glass. She stirred it quickly, drunk it, turned to Chuck, "The same as Jesus." A smile came to her face as she danced around the room.

"Oh my god! She's drugged you!" Chuck dragged Jim out the door.

Christopher Charles

Night

At the airbase on Pad #2 Meade stood by the four helicopters as his men remain standing in formation.

"For the last time I said board these helicopters," Meade shouted.

"We're waiting for Lucky Seven," Corporal Digs said.

"We've waited for him. He's not showing, so board!"

"We need to have him pray for us."

"I'll pray for you," Meade shouted, "God get these men aboard these helicopters before I kill them myself. There's your prayer. Now move it."

Digs moved slowly towards the helicopter. He looked around desperately.

Meade stepped beside him, yelling, "Move it!"

Digs quickly jumped aboard the helicopter. The others followed his lead and boarded.

Lucky Seven

Chuck, driving back to the base, used his free hand to talk into his radio mike. Jim remained wide-eyed beside him staring straight ahead.

"Grabowsky calling in."

Over radio speaker Bollinger yelled, "Where have you been? Your unit has already left."

"Taking care of some personal problems, sir. We really should take a bye on this one."

"Take a bye, are you wounded?"

"No sir, but Lieutenant Baughman has been through a lot emotionally. We really need to pass on this one, sir."

"This is not a social gathering, mister. This is war. We've got men down in the field of Lilies. Your unit is going in to relieve. Every spare helicopter is operating. No mister, there will be no bye."

"Yes sir."

"Don't bother checking in. Lift off and catch up with your unit. That's an order, mister."

"Yes sir. We will be there in ten."

Christopher Charles

At the airbase on PAD #3 Chuck pulled the Jeep up beside the lone helicopter #7. He jumped out and guided the staggering Jim aboard.

In the field of lilies four helicopters landed between four flares. The soldiers jumped from the helicopters. Overhead missiles came screaming in. One helicopter took a hit before everyone was out. Another helicopter managed to lift off before it took a hit. It dropped in a ball of flames. The third one remained on the ground until it is empty. Meade looked up at the pilot and whirled his fingers. The helicopter lifted off.

Meade turned to his stun men, yelling, "Form a firing line! Move it! Form a firing line, or you won't be going home."

Meade pushed anyone walking into the darkness. Wounded men were on the ground moaning around him. He reached for his radio, yelling, 'We have wounded. We took a direct hit coming in. I've got men down all around me."

Over the speaker phone, Captain Bollinger said, "Lucky Seven's on his way in. He should be there in five."

"Lucky Seven! About time our luck turned." He replaced his radio, and followed his men, shouting, "Lucky Seven's on his way. Give them hell! Lucky Seven's coming!"

The firefight became more intense in the darkness.

Meade stumbled into a body by the burning chopper. Dropping to his knee, he found Corporal Digs badly wounded. He took the corporal's hand.

Digs looked up at him, "Luck Seven's coming."

"Yes soldier, he'll be here in a minute."

"Thank you, Jesus."

Meade wiped a tear and quickly stood.

A jubilant soldier came running back out of the darkness, shouting, "They're running! They're running!"

Meade grabbed the Jubilant Soldier by his shirt, and yelled, "What's going on?"

"When you yelled Lucky Seven is coming, they broke and ran."

Meade looked around at the incoming soldiers, yelling, "Then let's get these wounded grouped for loading."

Meade's heard Chuck's muffled voice over the radio. Meade jerked the mike out, yelling, "Repeat!"

Over radio speaker Chuck said, "Helicopter number 7 overhead waiting landing instructions."

The wounded men around Meade give up a cheer.

Into the radio, Meade said, "Placing flares."

From the windscreen of the #7 helicopter the fading flames of the helicopters below appeared. Two flares toward the trees outline the landing site.

"Bring her down just east of the flames," Meade said.

"We're coming down!"

The whirling blades of the helicopter barely missed the tree branches going in. It rocked badly back and forth, but it managed to land in the space outlined by the flares and smothering helicopters.

Lucky Seven

"Let's get them aboard," Meade yelled

Chuck appeared at the door and directed the loading of the wounded soldiers. When the last one was aboard, he looked at Meade.

Meade whirled his fingers. Chuck disappeared inside. The soldiers on the ground watch as #7 helicopter lifted off. It veered away from the flames. The whirling blades struck the trees twenty feet above the ground, chopping parts of the whirling blades.

A body falls out of the helicopter's open door.

The helicopter managed another two hundred feet, but the chopped blades cannot lift the helicopter further, and dropped to the Earth landing on the smothering helicopters. It bursts into flames and exploded.

Meade and his men run toward the flames.

Jim's body laid on the ground beside the burning inferno. He slowly reached for a lone lily in front of him. He saw a vision of Crystal wearing a white flowing dress running towards him through the field of Lilies.

"Jim! Jim!" She cried out to him.

Christopher Charles

Jim's hand was almost around the lily, when he was jerked over on his back. He looked up at Meade holding him.

"Crystal! Crystal!" Jim said softly.

Meade lifted him close and smelled him, "Local brew!"

Jim continued in his hypnotic state, saying softly, "Love you. I love you."

Meade looked at Jim's blank stare, "Damn! You're on something." He threw him to the ground and drew his weapon. He pointed it at Jim's head, yelling, "Damn you! Damn you! I should shoot you, but I'll only be doing you a favor. You're going to regret this mister." He replaced his weapon, yelling, "One survivor over here."

Two Weeks Later

In the war room the officers and Meade sat around the table. Colonel Hardgrove was at one end with Matthews at his right side taking notes. Jim sat at the other end with his legal officer, Captain Stone.

Lucky Seven

Captain Stone was black and all business. He dropped his briefcase on the table for effect and opened it.

Colonel Hardgrove tapped his gavel on the table lightly, "The court martial of Lieutenant Baughman will commence. Captain Stone will conduct his defense." He turned to Jim, and continued, "You understand we can sentence you to be shot or set you free with an honorable discharge. You cannot remain in the army."

"Yes sir."

"What are the charges Corporal?" Colonel Hardgrove asked.

Corporal Matthews picked up the papers in front of him, "Flying while drunk and under the influence of the drug opium leading to the death of Lieutenant Grabowsky and eight enlisted men."

"How does the defendant plea, Captain Stone?" Colonel Hardgrove asked.

Captain Stone patted Jim on the shoulder, stood, "Guilty, but with special circumstances that should be taken into consideration."

Christopher Charles

"You shall mark the defendant as guilty, but with special circumstances to be considered," Colonel Hardgrove said.

Captain Stone continued, "Lieutenant Baughman was not aware he was drugged. He had just narrowly escaped death when two bombs were dropped on his church. It killed his total congregation including a local boy he was very close to. The bombing was not accidental as the record tries to show."

Colonel Hardgrove turned to Bollinger, "Captain Bollinger, can you elaborate on this?"

Bollinger worked his cigar around in his mouth, sat further back in his chair, "Hell no, it wasn't accidental. His congregation was VC, and his church was their ammunition dump. They were getting ready to make a raid on the base. We had no choice. Beside it was a good body count."

Captain Stone looked hard at Bollinger, "You didn't make Lieutenant Baughman aware of this, did you?"

"I got him out of there, didn't I?"

"But in what kind of mental frame? You want a man to watch those he loves die and expect him to perform his duties that require all his facilities to work properly."

"He does his job like the rest of us," Bollinger said. "We didn't tell him to take opium and fly. That was his decision."

Captain Stone reached into his briefcase and withdrew a piece of paper, "Maybe not." He handed the paper down the table for the officers to see, "I have a confession here from the only survivor of the village, an Old Woman. She said she drugged him without him knowing it. After that point he was no longer in command of his actions."

"He managed to fly his helicopter, didn't he?" Bollinger retorted.

"We don't know he flew it."

Sergeant Meade yelled out, "He knew!"

Hardgrove tapped the table with his gavel, '|"There will be no more outburst, Sergeant, or you will be cleared from these proceedings." He turned to Jim, "Now, Lieutenant Baughman, can you add to this?"

Jim stood with the help of Stone. He raised his head slowly and looked at Hardgrove, "I don't remember anything after Jesus left me and Taylor died."

"Captain Bollinger, you questioned the Old Woman who drugged him. Did you find out why?"

Bollinger leaned forward, looked hard at Jim, "She said it was to keep him from flying. She knew there was going to be reprisals from our bombing. He's been healing the VC for some time."

Meade clearly emotional, stood, and waited for Hardgrove to recognize him.

"Okay Meade, what do you have to add?"

"The firefight stopped when the VC heard Lucky Seven's helicopter was coming."

Captain Stone moved beside Jim, shouting, "I object! This court martial is not about aiding and abetting."

"It can be anything we choose it to be," Colonel Hardgrove said. "We will know the truth here."

Lucky Seven

"You won't be getting it from the Sergeant," Stone said. "He has always disliked the Lieutenant."

"Overruled," Coronel Hardgrove said. "You will continue Sergeant Meade."

"He psyched my men out by praying for them. They came back without a scratch. It wasn't because he prayed for them either. It's because the VC were following his orders. He's been controlling this base by making my men believe he has some kind of link with God. You see the results. Three quarters of my squad dead or wounded."

Colonel Hardgrove turned to Jim, "Lieutenant Baughman would you like to comment. You do not have to incriminate yourself, but it might help to clear things up."

Captain Stone placed his hand in front of Jim, "You do not need to respond. This court martial is not about that, but it will be if you respond."

Jim pushed Stone's arm away, "I only did what Jesus allowed me to do. I healed those that were hurt or sick, and I prayed for Sergeant Meade's men to be safe."

"Did you heal the VC lieutenant?" Colonel Hardgrove asked.

"I just healed when I felt his energy inside of me. It's gone now. I will not be healing anymore."

"You didn't answer my question."

Captain Stone moved Jim back, stepped in front of him, "Is this court martial willing to go on record saying Lieutenant Baughman was capable of healing people without medical support?"

Hardgrove quickly looked around the table. The officers refused to respond. He turned back to Stone, "This court martial will deal only with the deaths of Lieutenant Grabowsky and eight enlisted men."

"Then let's look at the facts." Captain Stone said, "Lieutenant Baughman flew into an area marked safe by Sergeant Meade. This is not the first time the Sergeant's poor judgment has taken a pilot's life."

Meade jumped to his feet yelling, "The other helicopters made it in all right."

"By landing further away from the trees," Stone said.

Lucky Seven

"They weren't drugged out of their mind," Meade shouted. "I've seen him fly. The trees weren't his problem."

Hardgrove pounded the table, "You will be seated, Sergeant. You are out of order."

Meade sat down and glared at Stone.

"Sergeant Meade is not on trial here," Colonel Hardgrove said.

Stone adjust his coat, looked down, and quietly said, "Maybe he should be." Then he cleared his throat, looked straight at Hardgrove, "Then these proceedings against Lieutenant Baughman should be dropped. He was drugged by an outside source beyond his control at a time when he was emotionally distraught. Who actually flew the helicopter remains suspect. We all know Lieutenant Grabowsky was night blind and could not have seen the trees. He should not have been in that helicopter to start with."

He paused, looked around the table, and then continued, "If you wish to push the abetting issue you will have to admit the healing abilities of Lieutenant Baugman exist."

Christopher Charles

Hardgrove squirmed in his seat and looked at the others. None of them looked at him. He turned back to Stone, "It is not the intent of this court martial to say Lieutenant Baughman has the power of God in his hands to heal. Realizing this will be his defense, I see no other option here then to declare him innocent of any wrongdoing and discharge him immediately from further duty. Is that agreeable, Counselor?"

"Honorable discharge?" Captain Stone asked.

"Agreed! Then this court martial is closed." Hardgrove tapped his gavel on the table. The men around the table quickly left the room. Jim and Stone remained alone.

Jim shook Stone's hand slowly, "Thank you for your help."

"It wasn't me. They were dirty, and they knew it. It was self-preservation that won."

Later

Jim was in the barracks. He was still in uniform, and slowly packed his spare military clothes into his duffle bag.

Lucky Seven

Novak knocked on the open door, entered, and asked, "Mind if I come in?

Jim shrugged his shoulders.

Novak came up beside him with his arms full of newspapers, "Have you seen the papers lately?"

"No, I'm not interested. It's finished. I'm going home. I can't heal anymore."

"Then you haven't read them?" Novak asked as he threw the papers on the bed. He picked up one set and reads it, "God forsakes Lucky Seven. He kills nine."

Pause:

"That's one, here's another, "Lucky Seven falls to Satan's drugs and kills nine."

Pause:

"It gets worse. You want to hear more?"

Jim waved his arm and turned away.

"Sorry, it's going to be tough. You might do better by not going home."

"I'm going home. Crystal's there. They gave me an honorable discharge." Jim said closing his duffle bag and tying it up.

"They didn't do you any favors. It would have been better if they had found you guilty and punished you."

"That's better?"

"They crucified Jesus because they found him innocent, didn't they?"

A Jeep appeared outside with two Military Police inside.

Jim looked out the window, turned to Novak, "That's for me. Are you coming this time?" Jim asked swinging his duffle bag on his shoulder. He headed for the door.

"No, I'm being pulled off your story unless you can give me something new to print."

Jim stopped, wiped a tear from his eye, "I don't remember a thing. God, I wish I did." He turned and disappeared out the door.

Novak walked to the bed, picked up another paper, and read it, "Crystal Hundly lost church due to Lucky Seven scandal."

Lucky Seven

He picked up another paper and read it. "How can she love him when God doesn't?" He looked out the window and wiped a tear, "Sorry Jim, I couldn't read these."

11 Going Home

They transported Jim by a military cargo plane to Hawaii. He took a commercial flight from there to the Ontario International Airport. News of Jim's arrival leaked out. People began arriving carrying signs. Two groups began to form. One side was for Jim and the other side was against him. The security guards quickly arrived and forced the two groups apart.

People coming off Jim's plane had to work their way through the large crowd. Ducking their heads, they walked rapidly between the security guards and the signs.

One set of signs read:

"MURDERER!" "COMMIE LOVER!"

"SAVE THE ENEMY TO KILL OUR BOYS!"

Another set of signs read:

"GET OUT OF VIETNAM!" "WHY ARE WE KILLING BABIES?"

"HEAL THEM NOT KILL THEM!"

Jim, wearing his uniform, appeared carrying his duffle bag on his shoulder. The crowd saw him.

Crowd One: yelled: "Murderer! Murderer!"

Crowd Two: yelled: "We believe! We believe!"

Crowd One pushed into Crowd Two forcing them back and knocking down their signs.

The security personnel quickly closed in around Jim and led him off between the two crowds.

A Big Man from Crowd One, wearing an army T-shirt and a Nazi arm band, pushed his way between the guards and spat into the Jim's face.

Jim wiped it off and disappeared down the hall. The crowd tried to follow the Big Man, but the security guards moved in quickly and forced them back.

"Commie lover!" The Big Man yelled, "Dirty Commie lover!"

A taxi was waiting by the curb with his trunk open. Jim came out the double doors with a security officer on each side of him. The security officers carrying Jim's duffle bag, threw it in the trunk and slammed the lid. The other security officer shoved Jim in the taxi and waved him on.

The crowd erupted from the doors as the taxi speeds away.

The Taxi Driver remained silent while he maneuvered through the traffic. When he reached the freeway, he relaxed, "There, I lost the lot of them."

"Sorry about the mess," Jim said.

"Yeah, I bet you are. Where to?"

"Pasadena, I'll tell you where when we get there."

The taxi sped up.

Lucky Seven

Forty Minutes later

The Taxi pulled up to the street curb beside the long driveway to Crystal's house. The driver turned around, "That will be fifty-two dollars."

Jim pulled out his wallet and only found a twenty. He handed it to the driver, "I have money in my duffle bag."

When he stepped out of the taxi to retrieve it, the taxi suddenly took off leaving him stranded.

"Hey!" Jim yelled, "My duffle bag! My money!"

The taxi picked up speed and disappeared around the corner.

Jim watched. Slowly he turned and began walking up the driveway. He was hoping Crystal might be here. He has not been able to contact her since she changed her phone number to avoid the reporters. He had stored his motorcycle at her mother's house, and the other reason he had come here. He reached the front door, rang the bell, and waited. He saw someone glance out the window. Then suddenly the door opened, and Mrs. Hundly was standing in front of him.

"What are you doing here?"

Christopher Charles

"I come to pick up my motorcycle and to see Crystal."

"I sold your motorcycle. I was tired of it taking up space in my garage. I gave the money to Crystal."

Jim stepped back, "Where can I find Crystal?"

"Nowhere! You have hurt her enough. Your marriage is a sham. I'm getting it annulled. Because of you she has lost her position at the church."

Jim dropped his head, backed away, "I still need to see her."

Mrs. Hundly stepped forward yelling, "If you find her, Reverend Gottschalk will have you arrested. He has a restraining order out on you. She's too good for the likes of you."

"I am very sorry for hurting everyone, please forgive me."

"How can one forgive you when God himself can't," Mrs. Hundly yelled. "You had his precious gift, but you chose to give it to the enemy. Now your best friend is dead, and eight others had to die for you. You're scum! You have always been scum!"

Jim turned and walked down the long driveway.

A Week Later Late in the Afternoon

Jim was walking along the dairy road towards the Grabowsky's house. The road was narrow with deep six-foot ditches on each side for the runoff water. His uniform was soiled, and his hair and beard were longer. He has been working his way here for a week. Without money he has been forced to live on the street sleeping where he could and looking for food in the dumpers behind the Mc Donald stores. He heard they threw out hamburgers after they become cold. He found they did not throw out all that much.

He walked up the long driveway towards the house. He saw Neil sitting in a chair on the front porch staring out over his dairy.

He saw Jim approaching, "There's nothing for you here, son."

Jim stopped at the bottom of the steps, looked up, "I wanted to tell you how sorry I am about Chuck."

Christopher Charles

"Sorry" don't bring him back." Neil's tears flowed. He wiped them, lifted his hand, and continued, "All of this was to be his, but he wanted to fly. Now he's dead... I worked hard for fifty years... All for nothing."

He paused, turned to Jim, "You took him away, so 'sorry' don't quite cut it, does it, son?"

Jim turned, and walked away.

Mary came to the screen door, "You sent him on his way?"

"He's gone."

"I called Ken at the Sheriff's Office."

"Now, you didn't have to go and do that."

"His drugs killed our son, and he's still walking around free."

"He healed Aunt Martha, didn't he?"

"The cost was too high."

Jim walked along the narrow road. He remained on the blacktop to avoid the deep drainage ditch beside it. A Sheriff Patrol car slowly passed him. It stopped, turned around, and pulled up beside him.

Jim stopped walking and watched the two Sheriffs step from their patrol car with their sticks. He raised his hands up as they began to beat him with their sticks. He falls and rolled into the ditch beside the road.

Jim remained in the ditch with his head barely out of the muddy water. He started to move his arms and stopped.

A vision appears:

He was seeing the night of the helicopter crash:

Hands were forcing him into the jump seat behind the pilot seat next to the open door. The helicopter lifted off. The flares on the ground become smaller as the two burning helicopters moved into view. He unbuckled his seatbelt, stood, turned toward the cockpit yelling, "Chuck! Chuck! What are you doing?"

The helicopter jerked upward and back throwing Jim out the open door. The ground came up fast-the vision went blank.

Christopher Charles

Jim shook his head clear and looked up at Ken, one of the waiting Sheriff Officers.

"Come on, get up here," Ken yelled down, "We're not through. Chuck was like a brother to me."

Jim slowly climbed the embankment. He covered his head the best he could as the beating continued. Finally, they threw him into the patrol car, and drove off. Jim was bleeding in many places and his body was hurting.

They arrived at the Sheriff's Station and Jim was taken inside. The cell door was opened, and Jim was thrown inside. He landed in a heap on the only bunk with his uniform torn and dirty. Two other inmates continued to lean against the far wall looking at him.

Five in the Morning

The Big Man wearing the army T-shirt from the airport a week ago entered the cell block yelling. A Sheriff Deputy behind him unlocked Jim's cell door.

The Big Man was pushed inside the cell complaining, "It wasn't my fault this time. The guy asked for it. I just helped him out."

Lucky Seven

The Sheriff Deputy locked the cell door, "Yeah. Yeah. That's why the man is in the hospital with a broken jaw."

Holding the bars, the Big Man yelled at the departing officer, "It ain't my fault he got in the way." The Big Man whirled around and noticed Jim lying on the bed. "Who's this in my bed?"

He pulled Jim from the bed, threw him to the floor, "I know who you are. You're that Commie lover. You heal them, so they can kill our guys." Then turning to the other inmates in the cell, he yelled, "Pick him up. This could turn out okay."

Prisoner One went to Jim, looked up at the Big Man, "Maybe you should leave him alone."

"I said pick him up!"

The other inmate pushed Prisoner One aside and lifted Jim from the floor. The Big Man shoved Jim against the wall. Jim's face was full of cuts and bruises.

The Big Man analyzed Jim, "Gees! Looks like someone's beat me to it." The Big Man released Jim allowing him to fall forward, "Go ahead. Heal yourself. I want my turn."

Christopher Charles

"I can't heal anyone anymore," Jim softly said.

Sheriff Deputy Ken entered the cell block, unlocked the cell, "Out of there Baughman. Grabowsky isn't pressing charges."

The Big Man seeing his prize being take from him, yelled, "Wait, I haven't finished."

"You're finished. Come on Baughman," Ken said. "You're being released."

Jim steady's himself and stumbled towards the door.

The Big Man lashed out with his foot and struck Jim in the left leg. A loud snap sent Jim to the floor in pain.

"There, now the Commie lover can go." The Big Man said.

Ken quickly entered the cell and backed the Big Man to the corner, saying, "That'll cost you an extra two months."

"It was worth it."

Jim worked his way to one leg and hobbled out of the cell.

Lucky Seven

Ken placed one hand under Jim's arm, took him out of the station and dumped him in the patrol car. Another officer climbed into the car and the patrol car drove to Riverside twenty miles away. In the car neither of the officers talked to Jim. When they reach Main Street, the patrol car slowed. When it reached an alley, it stopped.

Ken leaned back to Jim in the back seat, "Okay, out. This is where Old Man Grabowsky said to drop you."

Jim opened the door and climbed out.

"Sorry about your face," Ken said leaning out the window. "He didn't intend for you to come to harm. Said he had a vision. It wasn't you flying."

"Thanks for telling me. It means a lot."

"You sure your leg isn't broken?"

"I'll be okay," Jim said half standing on the sidewalk.

"Whatever you say," Ken said and closed the window. He motioned to the other officer and the patrol car left.

Christopher Charles

Jim looked around slowly as the Sheriff's car disappeared down the road. His eye caught a lit sign across the street that read:

EASTER SUNRISE SERVICE

FEATURING CRYSTAL HUNDLY

Tears streamed down Jim's face. He shook his head, stumbled into the alley, and falls into the shadows. A few bottles began to break in the alley, then it became quiet.

Twenty Minutes Later

Cars began to fill the street. They were turning into the parking lot across from the alley. People dressed in warm clothing walked along the sidewalk and turned into the parking lot.

On this side of the street Mrs. Taylor, a young black woman, and her six-year old son, Taylor Two, walked toward the alley and the crosswalk. She carried two chairs and a blanket. Taylor Two carried three lilies in a pot.

Taylor Two walked fast beside his mother, but he was having difficulty keeping up.

Lucky Seven

Hurry Taylor, or we'll be late," Mrs. Taylor said. "You know the best seating goes fast."

"I'm hurrying. This is heavy."

"I told you not to bring it."

"It's for Jesus."

Mrs. Taylor pulled him faster until she reached the crosswalk in front of the alley. She looked at the passing cars, but none of them would stop for her.

Taylor Two sat the heavy pot down beside him. He was unaware of Jim crawling out of the alley towards the pot of lilies.

Jim's hand touched the pot.

He had a vision:

Crystal, wearing a white flowing dress, stood in the middle of the lily field with her hands out, saying, "Jim, where are you?"

____

A brilliant flash and the vision was gone.

Christopher Charles

Taylor Two tried to pull his pot from Jim's grasp while Mrs. Taylor was beating Jim with her chair.

Taylor two was yelling, "Mommy! Mommy! He wants Jesus' flowers."

"Let go!" Mrs. Taylor yelled. She struck him again with the chair, yelling, "I said let go!"

Jim released the flower pot and rolled back to safety.

Mrs. Taylor quickly picked up the flower pot and gave it back to her son. She gathered her things, started for the street, "The nerve, come on Taylor, we can cross now."

Mrs. Taylor had Taylor Two by hand leading him across the street. Halfway across, she saw a truck bearing down on them. She jerked Taylor Two forward. It caused him to lose the flower pot.

"Mommy! Mommy! Jesus' flowers!" Taylor Two yelled. He pulled himself loose from his mother and ran back to the smashed pot. He reached for it when he saw the oncoming truck.

Jim laid face down on the sidewalk where Mrs. Taylor had left him. He heard the squealing

Lucky Seven

of the truck as it braked, and Mrs. Taylor as she screamed.

Mrs. Taylor laid over her son crying. The truck blocked the street causing a traffic jam. People came running from the other sidewalk and stalled cars. They gathered around the boy.

The Truck Driver pushed his way through the crowd, "Sorry Ma'am, I didn't see the boy."

Mrs. Taylor cried as the crowd becomes larger. She raised her head toward the dark morning sky, "Why Jesus? He is all I have. Why did you take him today of all days?"

A hand reached through the crowd. A body taking the shape of Jim crawled to the boy. Jim's hand reached under the boy and took him from his mother. The limp boy hanged over Jim's arms.

Mrs. Taylor cried as she released the boy to Jim, and said through her tears, "There's nothing you can do, he's dead."

Jim, holding the boy, prayed, "Jesus, Jesus please heal this boy. I feel your healing energy coming into my body. Let it touch him. Heal this boy. Please make him live again."

Christopher Charles

Taylor Two jerked in Jim's arms. The crowd gasped in amazement. Taylor Two opened his eyes and smiled at Jim.

Jim drew him closer, hugged him, "Thank you Jesus. Thank you."

The Truck Driver recognized Jim, "He healed him. He brought him back to life like my little girl. He's Lucky Seven! Look at his clothes. It's him all right."

Jim handed Taylor Two back to his mother. Mrs. Taylor hugged Jim and continued to cry.

"It's okay," Jim said. "Jesus has healed him."

Jim worked himself free of Mrs. Taylor's embrace and struggled to stand. She helped him hold his balance. Jim nodded and slowly limped back towards the alley.

"Please wait," Mrs. Taylor said.

Jim stopped and turned around.

Taylor Two continued to cling to his mother.

Mrs. Taylor reached down and picked up the flowers. She held them out to Jim, "Please take them."

Lucky Seven

Jim smiled and shook his head.

Crystal could be heard singing at the Easter Service across the street.

Mrs. Taylor ran and hugged Jim with her son still clinging to her. She handed Jim the flowers, "Please take them to her."

Taylor Two turned his head towards Jim, "It's okay. They're for Jesus."

Jim slowly took the flowers.

"Thank you, Lucky Seven," Mrs. Taylor said.

"I'm not Lucky Seven anymore," Jim said.

"Shhhh... Take them to her," Mrs. Taylor said. She turned and left carrying her son. The crowd quickly dispersed and headed toward the music and Crystal singing.

Jim remained standing and watched them all leave. Taylor Two waved to him from behind his mother.

Easter Sunrise Service was taking place on the football field. The bleachers were full of people facing the stage in the middle of the field.

Christopher Charles

People continued to fill the open grass on the playing field with their chairs and blankets.

A ten-foot aisle made of connecting rope marked off the middle of the field leading to the stage. Another twenty-foot aisle marked off the front of the bleachers and connects with the ten-foot aisle.

Taylor Two was clinging to his mother as she carried the two chairs and blanket. They follow the other people down the middle aisle.

Crystal was on stage singing. She was wearing a long flowing white dress. She was unaware of those around her.

Ushers with headphones directed Mrs. Taylor to a spot next to the aisle. The usher helped her with her two chairs, but Taylor II refused to leave his mother's lap.

Victor Novak, coming up the aisle, pointed to the empty chair beside Mrs. Taylor. She nodded, and he sat next to her.

Neil and Mary Grabowsky walked up the aisle and place their chairs across from them.

Lucky Seven

The overcast sky left those in the bleachers and on the grass cold and shivering.

On the stage Gottschalk sat with Mrs. Hundly. The huge choir to the left of them was singing along with Crystal.

Mrs. Hundly whispered to Gottschalk. "I hope he doesn't show."

"If he does, he won't make it very far," He nodded to the usher searching the crowd, "I will not have him make a shamble out of Crystal and my comeback."

"She sings so beautifully. Why did she have to fall in love with him?" Mrs. Hundly asked.

Gottschalk patted her on the knee, "That's why God placed us here, my dear." He paused, and then said, "To protect her innocents."

Outside across the street a pair of legs slowly hobbled across the street. Cars honk, but the legs continued their slow process.

Jim entered the far end of the field with a group of other people. He tried to stay with them, but they were too fast for him. When he reached the bleachers, he found safety in the shadows and stopped to rest. He was breathing hard and holding the three lilies. His tattered uniform was barely recognizable. The tears over the dirt on his bruised face were visible. He looked like a street person.

People stopped in front of him looking for a place to sit. They hid him from the roving Usher-One going past.

Into his mike Usher-One said, "No uniforms yet. Maybe he's not coming."

Pause:

"Yes, I know what he looks like."

On stage Crystal was singing 'Amazing Grace, (Save a wretch like me).'

Jim joined a group when they started walking up the ten-foot wide aisle. He hobbled beside them, but they quickly outpace him leaving him alone in the middle of the aisle. He stopped a moment to rest his leg. He looked up at Crystal singing. He tightened his grip on his flowers.

Taylor Two, sitting on his mother's lap, noticed him first, yelling, "It's him Mommy. It's Lucky Seven!"

Lucky Seven

The Truck Driver noticed Jim, "It's Lucky Seven all right. I saw him heal that boy."

"Lucky Seven! It's Lucky Seven!" Others picking it up continue repeating it as the words, "Lucky Seven," moved rapidly through the crowd.

The ushers descend upon Jim.

Crystal stopped singing and looked down at Jim.

Gottschalk jumped from his chair, held Crystal by her arms, and prevented her from moving.

Mrs. Hundly ran up beside Gottschalk, "It's him all right. Why did that awful man have to come and ruin everything?"

Mary Grabowsky, sitting next to the aisle beside Jim, slowly stood, stared at Jim, "Oh dear Jesus what have we done?"

Taylor II left his mother and ran up beside Jim. He took Jim's free hand and led him forward. Mrs. Taylor goes after them.

Jim's bruised face filled with tears.

"I help you," Taylor Two said.

Christopher Charles

Jim took two steps forward and falls. Mrs. Taylor reached Jim. She tried to help him up, but he was too heavy.

Two ushers arrived and pushed Taylor two and his mother aside. They each took an arm and lifted Jim.

Crystal's tears flowed.

Gottschalk turned to the choir behind him and indicated they should continue to sing.

Mary Grabowsky wiped her tears and pushed her husband, Neil, out into the aisle, "Go help that boy, Mr. Grabowsky. We owe it to Chuck."

Neil stepped up beside the usher. He placed his big hand on the man's shoulder, squeezed hard, "I will take over from here, son."

The other usher looked at him a second until Victor Novak relieved him, saying, "He's my friend. I'll help him."

Both ushers stood back in bewilderment. More ushers came running from the back. People began stepping out into the aisle to block them.

Mary and Mrs. Taylor join the developing crowd. Slowly the whole mass moved forward

Lucky Seven

toward the stage. The aisle in front of them remained clear until they pass.

People left their seats in the bleachers and joined the crowd.

Crystal's tears continued to flow. She pushed Gottschalk hands from her arms and ran down the aisle towards Jim.

The crowd cheered!

The clouds opened a stream of morning SUNLIGHT caught Crystal's white dress flowing behind her. When she reached Jim, they embraced.

The sunbeam enlarged, but its intensity remained on Jim and Crystal.

Mrs. Hundly, tears flowing, pushed away from Gottschalk, and ran down the aisle toward Crystal and Jim, saying, "I'm sorry! I'm sorry! Please Jesus, forgive me. I didn't know."

Gottschalk bowed his head and followed Mrs. Hundly down the aisle. When he reached the crowd, he dropped to his knees and bowed his head.

The choir was singing: "He Lives! He Lives!"

Christopher Charles

Jim raised his head. His face HEALS.

Crystal hugged Jim. Her tears of joy flowed.

Jim held Crystal tight against him with his left arm. Neil Grabowsky and Victor Novak remained on each side holding Jim steady.

Mary Grabowsky worked her way through the crowd until she touched Jim. Mrs. Hundly touched her daughter, and Taylor Two clung to Jim's legs.

Jim raised his hand holding the lilies into the air, "Forgive them father. Forgive them."

The song: "He lives", became LOUDER.

THE END